Born and raised on the Wirral Peninsula in England, **Charlotte Hawkes** is mum to two intrepid boys who love her to play building block games with them and who object loudly to the amount of time she spends on the computer. When she isn't writing—or building with blocks—she is company director for a small Anglo/French construction company. Charlotte loves to hear from readers, and you can contact her at her website: charlotte-hawkes.com.

Also by Charlotte Hawkes

The Army Doc's Secret Wife
The Surgeon's Baby Surprise
A Bride to Redeem Him

Hot Army Docs miniseries

Encounter with a Commanding Officer
Tempted by Dr Off-Limits

Discover more at millsandboon.co.uk.

THE SURGEON'S ONE-NIGHT BABY

CHARLOTTE HAWKES

MILLS & BOON

First published in Great Britain 2018
by Mills & Boon, an imprint of HarperCollins*Publishers*
1 London Bridge Street, London, SE1 9GF

Large Print edition 2019

© 2018 Charlotte Hawkes

ISBN: 978-0-263-07810-7

33421498 MIX
Paper from
responsible sources
FSC
www.fsc.org FSC® C007454

This book is produced from independently certified FSC™ paper to ensure responsible forest management. For more information visit www.harpercollins.co.uk/green.

Printed and bound in Great Britain
by CPI Group (UK) Ltd, Croydon, CR0 4YY

To Monty & Bart.

You make me laugh louder
and love deeper.

xxx

CHAPTER ONE

WITH MOUNTING HORROR, Archie stared out of the open aeroplane doors and three thousand five hundred feet down to the ground below her. As the penultimate static line jumper prepared to take his step out of the back of the plane, terror pinned her to the hard deck of the aircraft.

'You're up next, Archie.' Her instructor's words were more seen than heard as he yelled over the roar of the engines and the rushing wind.

'I can't. I can't do it,' she muttered desperately, but the sound was whipped away, unheard. Thankfully.

Throughout her entire life, those had been the only words her beloved air force father had ever flatly refused to hear... *I can't.* She glanced down at her colourful 'Make Cancer Jump' skydiving suit and felt a hot prickle in her eyes.

Guilt and regret; they had made terrible companions these last five years.

Whatever had happened to the bold, fun-loving, spirited Archana Coates of old? Even of six years ago? Back then she and her father would have jumped out of that door without a second thought. Now here she was, glued to the deck, unable to even inch her way forward.

She didn't dare look over her shoulder. She was the last of her group of static line jumpers but there was still half a planeload of tandem skydivers all ready to ascend to their required altitude of ten thousand feet. They were just waiting for her to go.

He was waiting for her to go.

Kaspar Athari.

She'd tried to ignore him from the moment she'd spotted him that morning across the vast chasm of the training hangar. Just as she'd ignored the way something had kicked in her chest, and if she hadn't already known it had died the same day her father had—almost five years ago to the day—she might have been fooled into believing it was her heart.

Kaspar. The boy who had burst into her family's life when she'd been six and he'd been almost eight, and had turned things upside down in the best way possible. For the seven years he hadn't just been her brother Robbie's best friend. He'd also been like a second brother to her, spending every school holiday from their boarding schools—thanks to Kaspar's money and her own father's career in the air force—with her family.

Or at least...mostly like a second brother. Even now, even here, she could feel the hot flush creep into her cheeks at the memory of childish crush she'd had on him that last year. She'd been thirteen and it had been the first year she'd been acutely aware that Kaspar wasn't a brother *at all*.

The same year his narcissist Hollywood royalty mother had finally tired of her latest husband and dragged herself and her son back to the States in the hope of kick-starting both their careers. But, though having once been one of the most heartbreaker child actors in Hollywood, thanks to a combination of his stunning blonde British mother and his striking, dark-haired Persian father, somewhere along the line Kaspar had turned his back on the industry.

Now he was a top surgeon who risked his

life in former war zones and on the battle-field. Saving civilians and soldiers alike. Winning awards and medals at every turn, none of which he appeared to care a jot about. With the press hanging on his every choice.

'The Surgeon Prince of Persia', the press had dubbed him, as much for his bone-melting good looks as for his surgical skill.

And even though she'd devoured every last article, had known he split his time between the US and the UK, had seen the Christmas card and US Army antique he'd sent her avid collector father every year without fail, she'd never seen Kaspar again in person. Until now.

Not that he'd even recognised her after all these years.

'Archie. Are you ready?'

Snapping her gaze back up to her instructor, who was still smiling encouragingly, she shook her head, half-incredulous that, even now, even here, Kaspar Athari had managed to consume her thoughts so easily. Especially when she hadn't thought of him very much at all over the intervening years.

Yeah, a voice inside her scoffed. *Right.*

But right now wasn't the time to go there. This skydive wasn't about him. It wasn't about anyone. Just herself. Just the fact that she'd spent the last five years, ever since her beloved father's death, ricocheting from one disaster to another, and today that all stopped. It was time. She just needed to make that leap. Literally.

Edging forward she somehow, miraculously, managed to summon the strength to push herself off her seat onto the metal floor, closer to the open hatch, and peer nervously down again.

The wind ripped at her, as though it could pull in even more different directions.

'I ca…' She began to mutter the refusal again but this time something stopped her from completing it.

It was time to regain her dignity. The life she'd somehow put on hold for the past five years since her father's death. In fact, almost five years to the day since her fearlessness had seeped out of her like a punctured rubber dinghy in the middle of a wide, empty ocean.

'I can do this,' she told herself fiercely. Out loud. Safe in the knowledge that no one could hear her over the roar.

She wanted to make the jump. She *needed* to make it. Five years of mistakes and disappointments had to end today. From her marriage, which had been doomed from the start, to the baby daughter she had lost at eighteen weeks. Even the baby that her ex-husband and his new wife would bring into the world barely a month or so. It was time to stop being a victim. To erase this weak, pathetic shadow of a person that she'd somehow become and rediscover the fierce, happy woman she'd once been.

Sitting on the cold, metal floor, paralysed with fear, wasn't part of the plan. And she hated herself for it. She reached out her arms and tried to shuffle across the floor on her bottom, but despite her best efforts her body refused to comply.

'I *have* to do this,' she choked out, desperately willing herself to move.

She was letting people down. She was letting herself down. She felt exposed, vulnerable, worthless.

Her head snapped around at the movement in her peripheral vision to see Kaspar edging his way through the plane. As if he knew exactly what was going on. As if the last fifteen years were falling away and they were once again the teenagers they'd been when she'd last seen him. As if he was still every inch the superhero he'd always been to her, even when she'd been nothing more than the annoying kid sister.

She should be more shocked. Shouldn't she?

He couldn't be coming to her aid. He wasn't that boy any more.

So what was hammering in her chest harder than the vibration of the aircraft engines? Had he recognised her after all?

'Everything okay?' he yelled. Concerned but with no trace of recognition.

Archie stared helplessly, attempting to shake off the irrational hurt that needled her. Why *would* he recognise her? It had been fifteen years and she'd liked to think she no longer looked *quite* like the gangly kid she'd been when he'd last seen her. It wasn't even as though her name would mean much to him, even if he could hear it over the roar of the engines. Archie was a name she'd only settled on in her later teens, and she doubted he'd ever even realised her name was Archana. Like her family, he'd only ever called her 'Little Ant', in reference to the ant farm she'd had as a kid, and the way she'd been so proud of her undaunted, determined little pet colony.

He moved closer, his mouth nearer to her ear so that she imagined she could even feel his breath.

'You want to jump?'

'I *have* to jump, but...' she choked out quietly, not sure whether he could read her lips.

He nodded curtly in response, before turning to her instructor.

'She can come with me. I was doing a tandem jump but my guy didn't even make it onto the plane.'

So Kaspar was an instructor here? Of course he was. What did the press call him? *Playboy... surgeon...adrenalin junkie.*

Articles waxed lyrical about his trekking in the Amazon, skiing down avalanche-prone mountains, or diving off hundred-foot-high cliffs into sparkling tropical waters. Being a skydiving instructor on his weekends off would be a cake walk to someone like Kaspar.

'You need to change harness.'

'Sorry?'

She didn't mean to flinch as his hand brushed her shoulder. It was instinctive. Consuming.

Now that her instructor had closed the door for the plane to ascend another six thousand feet or so, it was possible to hear each other without having to shout so loudly over the engines or the wind.

'The tandem's easier than the static line, and

I'll run you through the basics, but you'll need to change harness.'

And then Kaspar was addressing her, for the first time in fifteen years. She stared at him intently, as though willing up some spark of recognition, even if it was only to realise she was the kid sister who'd bugged him and Robbie. The one who had tried to get her brother to let her in when Robbie had far rather push her out. The one who had taught her little words in Persian, and chastised Robbie when he'd taught her swear words.

She gazed and, for a moment, she thought he stared back. Holding eye contact that fraction longer than necessary. It was as though the very blood was stilling in her veins, her body hanging for a split second. Everything seemed to tilt, to change colour.

But then he looked away, searching for the right harness, and she realised that moment had only existed in her own head. She could only watch in silence as Kaspar busied himself with the kit, slipping them both into the adult equivalent of a forward-facing baby carrier then sitting, with her perched on his lap, like the other tandem jumpers left in the plane.

It felt surreal. Nothing about this moment remotely resembled the hundreds of naïve fantasies she'd nurtured—for longer than she cared
to admit—about how a conversation with him
would go if she ever saw him again.

She'd envisaged beautiful clothes, perfect
hair and make-up, and her sexiest smile. She'd
imagined making Kaspar gasp at what he'd
failed to see, right under his nose, all those
years ago. She'd dreamed about making him
chase her, just a little, before inevitably giving
in to some all-consuming desire. Her innocent,
wholly unrequited teenage crush finally blos-
soming into some movie-perfect moment.

She had *not* imagined being in an aircraft
in the most unflattering, unshapely skydiving
suit, which bunched around the crotch thanks
to her heavy harness, and, to cap it all off, too
frightened to even make her jump.

Well, she'd be damned if she was going to
bottle this one, too. She had to make this jump.
From ten thousand feet. With Kaspar.

She absolutely was *not* thinking about how
close they were going to be, strapped together
in a harness, her back pressed against his front.

Her blood was absolutely not racing away in

her body, leaving her feeling decidedly light-headed and clammy.

She was going to concentrate on the jump and be grateful for the second chance. She had to do this well.

For charity.

For her father.

For herself.

And not because Kaspar was going to be with her for every single spine-tingling nanosecond of it. *Truly.*

Abruptly, everything faded to a blur, from Kaspar sorting out her gear to going through rigorous checks that would ordinarily have been completed on the ground. And then they were ready. Waiting. Her back glued to his chest.

Somehow that inability to face him lent her confidence.

'Why are you doing this?' she asked suddenly, surprising even herself.

Kaspar frowned.

'Sorry?'

Despite the relative quiet of the plane now the hatch door was closed, one still had to speak loudly and clearly to be heard and her murmur hadn't been nearly loud enough.

'Why are you doing this?' she repeated, grateful that no one else would stand a chance of hearing.

'Why am I doing this?' Kaspar repeated slowly, as if checking he'd heard right.

But she knew that cadence. Realised it meant he was choosing his words carefully. It felt like a tiny victory. She still knew him. Or a part of him anyway.

'Like a lot of people up here today, I'm doing it in memory of someone.'

'Who?' The question was out before she could swallow it back.

She could picture his face tightened, his jaw locked. So familiar even after all these years. The unexpectedness of it knotted in Archie's stomach and stopped her heart for a beat.

'We'll be at altitude soon.' He jerked his head to the door, clearly sidestepping her question, but she couldn't help it. She couldn't explain why but suddenly she needed to know.

'Who?' she insisted.

His jaw spasmed but, presumably because it was meant to be a charity jump and people had been sharing stories all day, he schooled his features into a neutral expression.

'His name was Peter. I knew him…a long time ago.'

He stopped curtly, as though it was more than he had intended to say. But it was more than enough for Archie.

Peter? Her father?

Archie shook her head, her lungs burning with the effort of continuing to breathe. He was doing this in memory of her own father? An odd sense of pride surged through her that even now, five years after his death, her big-hearted father still touched lives. And yet a sickening welling of emotion quickly snuffed out the pride. Kaspar clearly had absolutely no idea who she was. Despite all her earlier reasoning, that feeling of hurt, of rejection, coursed through her with all the power of a tsunami. She couldn't possibly hope to stop it, as illogical as she knew her reaction might be.

She opened her mouth, trying to find a way to tell him who she was. But at that moment the hatch door had reopened and her words were sucked out and into the ether before Kaspar had heard them. And as she sat there, her body feeling like lead, she was semi-aware of the other skydivers making their jumps even as her eyes blurred to everything around her.

The next thing she knew, Kaspar was hauling her to her feet, carrying out the final procedures, and then they were moving to the door, exiting the plane, dropping for what seemed like for ever but was probably no more than thirty seconds or so.

And without warning every thought, every emotion seemed to fall from Archie's mind, leaving her strangely numb.

At some point, it had to have been quite quickly, Kaspar tapped her shoulder to remind her to spread out her arms and legs in the freefall position as they rushed towards the ground, although it was as though the ground was rushing to them, her back pressed to his solid, reassuring chest. There was no chance for conversation up here, they could shout and yell and the other one would never hear them, and to Archie there was something freeing in that. For all intents and purposes she was alone, even if she could feel Kaspar's rock-like mass securing her. As the adrenalin coursed through her veins, pumping along like nothing could hold it back, it was as though the wind not only blew away the stiffness from her body but the fog that had clouded her mind for so long.

Too long.

Kaspar opened the chute at what Archie knew would have been around five thousand feet, the loud *crack* ripping through her entire being as they were yanked up into a more upright position, as if breaking her open and allowing the first hints of fear and anger and regret to seep out.

And then absolute silence.

Peace.

Her heart, her whole chest swelled with emotion.

They were still descending but, with the parachute above them now slowing their rate of descent, if she didn't look at the ground, it almost felt as though they were floating. Suddenly time seemed to stand still.

Another thrill rippled through her.

She remembered what it had felt like on that first jump with her father. The life she'd intended to have. The strength of character that used to be hers. And for a moment she felt that again. Free of any responsibility for opening the parachute, steering them to the landing zone, or even having to land safely, she felt her body relax for the first time in years. And the more her body let go of some of the tension it had bottled inside for too long, the more her mind also opened up.

Lost in her thoughts, she was almost startled when a thumb appeared in front of her.

'Okay?' he yelled, his mouth by her ear.

Instinctively, she thrust both her hands out in a double thumbs-up, nodding her head as vigorously as she could, and then he was offering her the paddles to try controlling the chute for herself for a moment.

She was about to shake her head when something stopped her. For a split second she could almost hear her father's voice in her head encouraging her to do it. Tentatively, she reached up and took hold, changing direction slowly at first, surprised at just how comfortable and natural it felt. Even six years on, it was as though her muscles had retained the training her father had given her.

'Were you really going to do tandem jumps today?' She twisted her head so he could hear her easier.

Kaspar nodded. 'I was subbing for another instructor friend of mine who's unwell today. Originally, though, I was going to sky surf. Peter would have loved that.'

He stopped again, clearly catching himself.

Archie thought back to the surfboards she'd seen in the hangar on the ground and smiled into the expanse of blue. Of course a simple skydive wouldn't be enough for adrenalin junkie Kaspar, but he was right, her dad would have loved it.

Bolstered, she tried a slightly trickier turn, surprised and delighted at how comfortable and natural it felt, things that her father had taught her coming back quicker than she might have anticipated. Again and again she steered the chute, going further, trying things out, wishing she had the skill to really push her boundaries. All too soon it was time to release the paddles back to Kaspar.

Almost as though he could read her mind, Kaspar steered them into a high-speed turn, a gurgle of laughter that she hadn't heard from herself in years rumbling through her and spilling into the silent sky. She revelled in the sound as Kaspar led them both into a series of high-speed manoeuvres that thrilled her beyond anything she'd hoped for.

They held such echoes of what she'd loved until recently. For a moment it was as though she could almost reach in and touch the spirited, strong girl she'd once been.

It was transitory. Archie knew that. Soon Kaspar would have to stop and once they landed this moment, this connection to her old self, would be lost.

But this jump had done the one thing she'd desperately wanted it to do. It had finally reminded her of the girl she'd once been and—however deeply buried that part of her may be—today had helped her to begin her journey back to the old Archie.

The biggest shock of all was that it wouldn't have happened but for Kaspar Athari.

He might have no idea who she was, and once this jump was done he'd be out of her life again. Maybe for another fifteen years. Probably for good. But she was grateful to him nonetheless. Part of her longed to reveal her identity to him, but part of her was afraid of ruining the moment.

She was still gazing at the scenery spread out beneath them like the most vivid green screen image, trying to decide, when a small explosion by a truck in a layby below them snagged her attention. They were still a little too high up to see much detail but a dark shape lay on the ground. Archie opened her mouth to speak but Kaspar was already steering the parachute around for a better look.

'Is that a person?' she asked tentatively after a few moments. 'Or bins? Or bags?'

'I can't be sure. Possibly a person.'

His grim tone only confirmed her fears. If it was a body, they would likely have been caught in the blast.

'They have ambulance crews on the ground at the fete,' she shouted.

'That's true but the fete's some way away, they won't have seen the blast we saw. And I know that stretch of road, it's on the route from the hospital and Rick's Food Truck is parked in that layby six days a week, popular with both weekday truckers and with weekend walkers, all looking for a hot bacon and egg bap. For me, Rick's sausage and tomato toasties are more than welcome after a long night shift.'

'So what's the plan?' she asked, knowing neither she nor Kaspar would have mobile phones on the jump.

The decisive note in her tone was something she hadn't heard in all too long.

'There's about a mile over the fields, as the crow flies, between the truck and the fete. If we land as close as we can to the layby we can check it out. If it *is* a person, I'll stay on scene while you run back and alert the medical crews at the fete. Understood?'

'Understood,' she confirmed, caught off guard by an unexpected flashback to a time when Robbie had come off his bike, trying to do some somersault trick, and had been lying deathly still on the ground.

She'd been beside herself, but Kaspar had taken control then much as he was now. Assessing, verifying, trying to assimilate as much pertinent information as he could. Kaspar had taught her a lot, even as a kid.

Just like her father had.

Right now, she suddenly realised, she felt more like her old self than she had for years. Who would have thought she would owe Kaspar Athari part of the credit for that?

CHAPTER TWO

KASPAR VAULTED OVER the hedge and through the field. A part of him was glad to be getting away from the girl—*Archie*, her instructor had called her—with her expression-laden eyes that seemed to see altogether too much. It made no sense and yet even through her obvious fear up there in the plane, every time she had fixed that clear gaze on him he'd been unable to shake the impression that she could see past the façade he'd carefully crafted for a drooling press over the years, and read his very soul.

If he'd actually had a soul. But that had been long shattered. As much by his own terrible mistakes as anything else. Not least the one night that had altered the course of his life for ever.

And yet he couldn't seem to shake the notion that this one girl—woman—almost *knew* him. As though she was almost familiar.

He told himself it was just the emotion of

the day. Five years since he'd heard Peter had passed away, the closest thing he'd ever had to a real, decent father figure. Who, even as a widower trying to hold down his air force career, had been more of a father *and* a mother to his son and daughter than either of Kaspar's own very much alive parents could or would ever have been.

Peter Coates had taught him that the volatile, physically terrifying marriage of his own parents wasn't normal or right. He'd taught Kaspar to handle his emotions so that he didn't lose control the way his own father had. The way his own mother had, for that matter.

Hearing about Peter's death had winded him. Along with the rumour that Robbie had subsequently sold the old farmhouse and emigrated to Australia. Kaspar could understand why. With both parents dead, Robbie, only twenty-five, and with that kid sister of his to look after, it made sense to have a completely fresh start. And yet somehow, knowing the Coates family no longer lived in that cosy, old, sandstone place with its roaring open fires, it had felt like the end of an era.

'Rick? Mate, can you hear me?' Kaspar shook

the memories off and called out with deliberate cheerfulness as he approached the figure lying on the ground, one eye half-closed and bloodied.

The extent of the blast damage made it almost impossible to recognise the man as Rick, but the man's build and clothing fitted. There was one way to tell for certain, though. Carefully, Kaspar ripped the man's shirt sleeve.

A clipper ship stared boldly back.

Rick. But he wasn't conscious. Pinching the man's side, Kaspar began a quick examination, surprised when Archie came running up not far behind him. Her intake of breath was the only acknowledgement that the dark shadow was indeed a person.

'Is it your friend Rick?'

'Yes. Get a medical crew,' he instructed.

'He might have a mobile,' she suggested hopefully, but Kaspar shook his head.

'He doesn't. Claims to hate them. So you'll just have to hoof it. Can you do that?'

'Yes.'

'Good. Tell them to alert the air ambulance and say we've got an unresponsive adult male, around fifty, with severe maxillofacial blast injury, including tissue loss of the right eye and nose and unstable maxilla. GCS three and his airway is going to need to be secured immediately.'

She recited it back clearly and competently despite the slight quake in her voice then left. Kaspar turned back to Rick. By the looks of it, the man was mercifully beginning to regain some degree of consciousness.

'Rick? It's Kaspar. Can you hear me?'

At least the older guy was making vague groaning noises now, even if he didn't appear to recognise Kaspar at all. He certainly couldn't seem to speak, although that was hardly a surprise. Keeping up light, breezy conversation, Kaspar concentrated on the injuries and the potential damage to the man's airway. If that collapsed, things would spiral downwards pretty damned fast.

Occupied, it felt like it was only minutes later when the helicopter landed and the on-board trauma doctor came racing over.

'Kaspar Athari.' The doctor nodded in deference. 'Your partner said it was you. I'm Tom. What have we got?'

'Adult male, around fifty years old. Name is Rick.'

'Rick the food truck guy? You're sure?'

'Sure enough.' Briefly, Kaspar tapped a bold, unusual tattoo on the man's upper arm. 'Approximately fifteen minutes ago he was changing a gas bottle on his food truck when it exploded, no witnesses except myself and my skydiving partner but we were too far away to see clearly. He appears to have been projected by the force and hit his face and neck on something, I would guess the vehicle bracket. There's tissue loss of the right eye and of the nose, unstable maxilla and suspected crushed larynx. Initially unresponsive, he's now producing sounds in response to verbal stimuli. GCS was three, now four.'

'And he's breathing?'

'For now,' Kaspar said quietly. 'But with the soft tissue swelling and oedema there's still a risk of delayed airway compromise, while haemorrhage from vessels in the open wounds or severe nasal bleeding from complex blood supply could contribute to airway obstruction.'

'Okay, so the mask is out, given the damage to his face, supraglottic devices are out because of his jaw, and intubation is out because if the blast caused trauma to the larynx and trachea, any further swelling could potentially displace the epiglottis, the vocal cords and the arytenoid cartilage.'

The trauma doctor ran through the list quickly, efficiently. He was pretty good—something Kaspar always liked to see.

'One more thing,' Kaspar noted. 'There's a possible cervical injury.'

'One p.m. So we've got a high risk of a full stomach after lunch, which means increased risk of regurgitation and aspiration of gastric contents. I could insert a nasogastric tube or I could apply cricoid pressure, but either of those procedures could worsen his larynx and airway injuries.'

At least the guy was thinking.

'Yes,' Kaspar agreed slowly, not wanting to step on anyone's toes. Ultimately, this was the trauma doctor's scene. He himself might be a surgeon, but today he was a skydiver on his day off. 'Still, I'm not confident that his airway will hold without intervention.'

'Can't intubate, can't ventilate,' Tom mused. 'Which leaves a surgical airway option. Tracheotomy or cricothyroidotomy.'

'I'd say so,' Kaspar concurred, thrusting his hands in his pockets to keep from taking over. The doctor was actually good, but Kaspar knew he'd be faster, sharper. It was, after all, his field of expertise.

It was the one thing that gave him value in this world. Every patient. Every procedure. They mattered. As though a part of him imagined that each successful outcome could somehow make up for his unthinking actions that one night with a couple of drunken idiots. As though it could somehow redress the balance. A hundred good deeds, a *thousand* of them, to make up for that one stupid, costly error of judgement.

But it never would.

Because it hadn't been merely a mistake. It had been a loss of control. The kind that was all too reminiscent of his volatile father.

The kind that Peter Coates had tried to teach him never to lose.

The memories burned brightly—too brightly—in his head. It must be why he was feeling so disorientated. He'd thought the jump would help, but jumping with that woman had somehow heightened it all.

A familiar anger wound its way inside him. Even now, all these years later. All his awards, his battlefield medals, the way the media lauded him meant nothing.

In many respects he was glad that Archie woman was gone. She was, for some inexplicable reason, far too unsettling. The way she'd looked at him on that plane. As though seeing past the playboy front and believing he would do the right thing and help her.

He couldn't explain it, but she didn't look at him the way almost everyone else in his life looked at him. She didn't look at him as though calculating what being with him would do for her career, or reputation, or fame. In fact, she'd looked at him with eyes so heavy with meaning he hadn't been able to stop himself from wondering what it was she'd seen. Why she made him feel more exposed than anyone had in long, long time.

It made no sense. And Kaspar hated things not making sense.

Just as he hated the part of him that had wondered whether, when this was over and the patient was safely on board the air ambulance, he might head back to the fete or the hangar and perhaps buy her a coffee. Or a celebratory drink that night.

For the first time in a long time the idea of a *date* actually made him feel…alive.

'Want to do the honours?'

Tom's voice broke into his thoughts.

'You're the on-duty trauma doctor.' Kaspar hesitated, fighting the compulsion to jump straight in, needing to be sure. Not to protect himself but to protect the hospital. He owed them that much. 'And you're good.'

'I am.' There was nothing boastful about the way the doctor said it. Simply factual. Exactly as Kaspar might have said it. 'But you're the oral and maxillofacial specialist, it's right up your street and this is a particularly complex patient. I can't afford to make a wrong move. If anyone is going to be able to stabilise him enough to survive the flight, it's going to be you.'

'Fine,' Kaspar acknowledged. It was all he needed to hear.

He bent his head to concentrate on the job he loved best, and pushed all other thoughts from his mind. He wouldn't think any more about Archie. He wouldn't be taking her for a drink that night. And he certainly wouldn't be attending the charity wrap party.

The party was in full swing and, predictably, people were crowding around him, from awed wannabe colleagues to seductive wannabe girl-friends.

But there was only one person from whom Kasper couldn't seem to drag his gaze.

It was ludicrous. So uncharacteristic. Yet it felt inexorable.

He hadn't been able to eject her from his thoughts since the skydive, however hard he'd tried. And he wasn't a man accustomed to failure—as a surgeon he had one of the highest success rates—which made it all the more incredible that banishing one woman from his thoughts was defeating him. If anything, with each day that passed she'd become more of a delicious enigma until he'd found himself powerless to resist coming here tonight.

Just on the off chance that he might see her again.

When was the last time a woman had done that to him?

Had *any* woman? Ever?

He tipped his head in consideration, finally allowing himself to give in to impulse.

Archie was stunning. Not necessarily in looks, although she was certainly very pretty, from her sexy pair of *look-at-me* heels to legs that seemed to go on for ever before they finally slipped beneath a short, Latin-inspired, tasselled dance dress number, showing off perhaps the shapeliest pair of legs he ever recalled seeing. He couldn't seem to help himself, but he practically imagined her wrapping them around his body as he sank into her, so deep that she wouldn't know where he ended and she began.

His body tightened just thinking about it.

Him. Kaspar Athari.

He had never wanted *any* woman quite like this.

He'd never *wanted* quite like this.

He'd had enough women throwing themselves at him on practically a weekly basis that he'd never had to lust after any woman quite so…*helplessly.* Not the most stunning supermodels, or the most worshipped Hollywood starlets. But he was lusting after this perfectly pretty, perfectly cheeky, perfectly ordinary woman. Who, it turned out, was to him most extraordinary.

A little like the woman who had been too frightened to do the static line jump but who, when steering the tandem jump chute with him, had displayed a skill and eagerness that had belied his initial conclusion that she was a novice.

Against all logic, Kaspar found himself fascinated.

There was a story there. *But what?* And why did he even care?

Sexual attraction was one thing. But this was something else. Something...*more*. Certainly more than the physical. She possessed a magnetism in the aura she gave off and the way people gravitated towards her. Especially— and Kaspar gritted his teeth at the thought— the other men on the dance floor. Was he the only one to notice how she danced and twirled, shaking and shimmying quite mesmerisingly, and yet all the while deftly kept her friend between herself and any would-be suitors?

As if the intensity of his stare had finally reached her, she lifted her head, met his gaze and froze. Even from this distance, in this light, he could see the sweetest bloom staining her cheeks and down the elegant line of her neck, her chest rising and falling rapidly in a way that had nothing to do with the fact she'd been dancing. Or perhaps it was just the vividness of his imagination. Remembering the way she'd flushed in the plane the other day.

Either way, he was certain she was consumed by the same greedy fire as he was. The fire that had brought him here tonight, against every shred of logic.

And then she moved, heading off the floor and away from him. His stomach lurched in a way that was all too alien to him and before Kaspar knew what he was doing, he had set his untouched drink down on the bar behind him and was shifting his feet, ready to move. Not prepared to lose her.

Abruptly, her friend caught her and pulled her back. He kept waiting for them to glance in his direction, maybe share a giggle, which he'd seen from women time and again. A part of him almost welcomed it. It might help to topple her from whatever invisible pedestal on which he'd set her, help remind him that she was a woman like any other.

But it didn't happen. If anything, Archie studiously avoided meeting his gaze again, and had clearly omitted to mention him to her friend, and her dignified discretion only seemed to add to her allure. Especially when she resumed dancing, only to be a little more self-conscious, a fraction stiffer than she had been before. It was the tell he needed, knowing now she was indeed equally attracted to him.

It should concern him more that it felt like such a victory.

Alarm bells were sounding but too faint, too distant to have the impact he suspected they should have had. To jolt him back to reality. To warn him that she didn't look like the kind of woman who did one-night stands. She looked like the kind of woman who did walks along beaches, and romantic meals, and talking until dawn. Relationships. *Love*. It was such bull.

He'd seen first-hand the toxic depths to which such emotions could plunge. His parents' explosive marriage had been equalled only by their acrimonious divorce. And him, in the middle of it all his life. Their pawn. The tool they'd used to goad and taunt each other. The burden they'd each tried to make the other one bear.

And not just his parents. What about his own explosiveness? That out-of-control side of him that had only had to emerge once to completely ruin someone's life. He'd sworn it would never happen again, and it hadn't. Some might call him emotionally detached, or unavailable. He wasn't. Where his patients were concerned he felt as much empathy as he could, for patient and family, without it impairing his ability to do his job. It was only in his personal life where he exerted such emotional...*discipline.*

So he did sex. He did fun. He did mutual gratification.

He didn't do intimacy and he didn't do complications.

Something told him that this Archie woman was both, and the best thing he could do, for both of them, would be to stay away.

Turning back to the bar, Kaspar picked up his drink and tried not to be irritated by the group of preening, simpering women who had begun to cluster around his part of the bar. It was about as easy as pretending he wasn't searching out blonde hair and a metallic shimmer in the reflection of the mirror behind the glasses.

Apparently, his skydiving butterfly was now edging her way off the opposite side of the dance floor. About as far away from him as she could get.

He didn't give himself time for second-guessing. For the second time that evening, he set his untouched drink down and gave in to temptation.

CHAPTER THREE

'ARCHIE, WAIT. SLOW DOWN. Where are you going this time?'

'Relax,' Archie cast over her shoulder, a bright smile plastered to her lips at her friend's typically bossy tone. 'I'm just going for a drink.'

Still, she didn't slow down in her quest to get off the dance floor and around to the other side of an enormous pillar that would shield her from Kaspar's view. No easy feat in the ridiculously high heels Katie had insisted on lending her to go with the seriously sexy metallic number her friend had also talked her into buying this afternoon.

It was years since she'd been out so called *clubbing it*—not that she'd ever had the time or inclination to go out all that often, neither was this charity wrap party exactly *clubbing it*—but, still, she hoped she hadn't looked too awkward and robotic out there on the dance floor. She'd felt fine…right up until she'd seen him watching her.

The minute she'd spotted him, her body hadn't quite felt her own. As though it wasn't completely under her control. Even now the memory of his eyes scanning over her left her blood feeling as though it was effervescing through her veins, making her entire body hum.

It was an unfamiliar, but not altogether unpleasant sensation.

Ducking behind the pillar, Archie pressed her back against the cool, smooth concrete and rested her hand underneath her breastbone. She could feel the tattoo her heart was drumming out, leaving her unable to even catch her breath. And it had nothing to do with the dancing. Oh, she'd tried to ignore him, especially when his usual harem had draped themselves around him and he'd barely had the decency to offer any of them the time of day.

But who could ignore Kaspar Athari?

'So, if you're getting a drink why are we the other side of the room from the bar?' Katie bobbed under her nose, her brow knitted.

'Hmm? Oh. I just…needed to catch my breath.'

It wasn't exactly a lie, but she might have known her old friend would see through it.

'Archie, you're about as jittery as a beachgoer trying to get across hot sand.'

'No, I'm not.'

Katie's eyes narrowed sharply.

'Is this about "the Surgeon Prince of Persia"?'

'I don't know what you're talking about,' she managed loftily, only for Katie to snort in derision.

'Yeah, sure you don't. He's been devouring you with his eyes all night and you've been lapping it up.'

'I have not,' Archie spluttered, her knotted stomach twisting and flipping. 'And it hasn't been all night. It has been half an hour at most.'

'Aha!' Katie declared triumphantly. 'So it *is* about the perennially sexy Kaspar Athari.'

'No…not at all…well, not really. That is… Why are you frowning? Aren't you the one who said I needed to get back out there and have fun, like we used to in uni? Like I did before my dad…died? Before I married Joe?'

She tailed off awkwardly as Katie pulled a face.

'I've said it before and I'll say it again, I al-

CHARLOTTE HAWKES 45

ways hated the way you changed when you married Joe. You went right into yourself. Nothing like the fun, sassy Archie I'd come to know.'

'It wasn't Joe who did that.' Archie wrinkled her nose. She'd tried a hundred times to explain it to Katie, but her friend had never quite understood. Still, she couldn't help feeling she owed it to Joe to try again. 'He was exactly what I needed at that time in my life.'

'I disagree.'

'I know you do. You remind me often enough.'

Still, there was no rancour in Archie's tone. In many respects it was buoying that her friend cared enough to do so. And Katie's wry smile of response revealed that she knew it, too.

'I just feel that, while he may not have intended to, Joe took advantage of the fact that you were young and naïve. You were grieving for your dad, and your brother and his new wife were half a world away.'

They were falling into a conversation they'd had a hundred times before, but it was impossible to stop.

'He didn't take advantage. It was mutually beneficial.'

Katie's eyebrows were practically lost in her

hairline, but at least she had the tact not to bring up any painful reminders of more than three years of failed pregnancy attempts. The miscarriage at eighteen weeks.

Agony seared through her. Black, almost debilitating.

Faith.

As though it didn't lacerate her from the inside out just *thinking* her unborn daughter's name.

She swayed dangerously.

Had it not been for the silent, supportive hand at her elbow, Archie was afraid she was about to tumble to the floor. She blinked at Katie gratefully. Unspoken, unequivocal support shone back at Archie. Bolstering her. Making her want to forget the fact that, barely a year after she'd lost her unborn daughter, Joe was expecting a baby with his new wife.

It hurt.

Though not, perhaps, in precisely the way Archie might have thought it would. She couldn't pinpoint it, but neither could she help suspecting that it had less to do with Joe than it ought to, and more to do with the simple pain that another woman seemed to find it so easy to have a baby while her own traitorous body hadn't been able to do the one thing she felt it had surely been designed to do.

'Fine, let's say it was mutually beneficial...' Katie conceded at length, though Archie could hear by her friend's tone that she didn't remotely believe that.

'You look like you've swallowed a bee.'

She couldn't help a chuckle, even it did sound half laugh, half choked-back sob. Katie valiantly attempted to ignore her.

'Mutually beneficial,' she repeated firmly. 'And you're right. Now is your time to get back the Archie I used to know. The one I admired so much that I used to wish I was more like you. The Archie who threw herself out of a plane today, for her father, for Faith, for a new start.'

'You make it sound so easy.' Archie smiled softly, the sadness she tried so hard to shake but couldn't still tiptoeing around inside her.

But she wanted to. And the jump today was the first time she'd felt she might actually be ready to do so.

Because of the jump? Or because of Kaspar?

Archie slammed away the unbidden thought in an instant but it was too late. It couldn't be *un*-thought. Instinctively, her eyes were drawn back to where Kaspar had been standing, staring at the pillar as though they could bore a path straight through it to see him.

It was pathetic.

But it was also the biggest vaguely positive reaction she'd had to anything or anyone in a very long time. And that felt strangely compelling.

Kaspar Athari, back in her life after all these years. He'd been her first, only crush. Except back then he hadn't even noticed her and so she hadn't had the guts to do anything about it. Suddenly, here he was again and this time he had certainly noticed her. It was as though she was being offered a second chance. It couldn't be just a coincidence, surely? It had to be *fate*. Either way, it was making her want to...*do* something. Anything.

She turned to Katie with as firm a nod as she could manage.

'Fake it till you make it, right?'

'Absolutely.'

It was easier said than done, but what the heck.

'Fine.' Archie sucked in a deep, steadying breath. 'Then if I'm going to...what did you say earlier this evening? Get back on the horse?

Then why not go all out with the infamous "Surgeon Prince of Persia"?'

Why did it feel easier to call him by his ridiculous nickname? Was it because it felt too close to home to call him Kaspar?

'Yes.' Katie didn't look remotely abashed. 'I did say that. But not with him. He'd gobble you up and spit you out. The man is pure danger.'

Seriously, how difficult could it be to dredge up a casual grin while simultaneously trying to stop her stomach from executing a perfect nose-dive?

'Maybe that's what I need?' she tried hopefully. 'A bit of danger.'

'Absolutely not.' Katie shook her head so vigorously her shiny halo of curls bobbed perfectly around her pretty face. 'No chance. There's absolutely no way I'm letting a guy like that get anywhere near you. Over my dead body. You can count on me for that.'

Archie frowned, confused.

'I've heard you drool over the Surgeon Prince a hundred times. Are you really saying you wouldn't go there after all?'

'Of course I would,' Katie scoffed loudly. 'Trust me, I'd be in there like a shot if the guy so much as squinted in my direction.'

'So he's okay for you, but not okay for me?'

Archie didn't know whether to feel insulted or honoured.

'He's not okay for you *right now*. If you were the old, fearsome Archie from back in uni, then I'd say go for it. *That* Archie could have handled a man like Athari.'

This was it. She could either go along with what her friend was saying, proving Katie right. Or she could show a little spirit. Like she had on that skydive. Not that she'd told Katie, who'd been occupied with her own charity water-polo match, about the tandem jump.

Archie blew out sharply.

'You know, I think I can handle one little prince.'

Katie opened her mouth, eyed her and closed her mouth again. A crooked smile that Archie knew so well hovered on her friend's lips.

'I do believe you mean it.'

'I do.'

Katie paused, considering.

'Then far be it from me to stop you. Okay, you know that sexy, dangerous scar across his jawline?' Archie nodded silently. 'Apparently it was the result of some big fight when he was younger.' Katie hugged her arm tightly and whispered in conspiratorial tones. 'You remember those massive Hollywood kung-fu, karate-style blockbusters he did as a seven- and eight-year-old?'

The Hollywood life he'd been only too desperate to run away from, Archie remembered. Not that she could say anything.

'Yes, I think so,' she hedged instead.

'Of course you have to know them. They were *huge*, until his mother apparently demanded too much money or riders or whatever and he got kicked out and replaced.'

The rumours didn't come close to the damage his volatile mother had caused. But she couldn't say that either.

'So you heard he got the scar on those films?' Archie tactfully changed subject.

Katie's eyes sparkled with excitement.

'No, the rumour I actually read somewhere was that the fight was down some back alley when he was about seventeen or something, and wasted after a drinking session. Apparently he was outnumbered five to one but he still beat their collective backsides. Juicy, isn't it?'

'Juicy,' Archie agreed half-heartedly.

The idea of the quiet, controlled Kaspar of

back then drinking, let alone fighting, was a complete anathema to her. No doubt a lie the press had spun to help them with their paper-shifting image of the playboy Kaspar. Not that he hadn't played his own stupid part to a T.

But the man in the media bore little resemblance to the boy she'd once known. And it was the latter who had stolen her adolescent heart.

Besides, she'd been there when he'd really got that scar, climbing the forty-foot oak tree outside Shady Sadie's house when he'd been fifteen. Or at least she'd been in the living room with her father when Robbie had raced back to say that a damaged limb had given way and Kaspar had fallen to the ground. He'd been carted off to the hospital with a few superficial cuts and bruises and that one deep gash. He'd worn it with all the pride of a battle scar, of course. Trust the media to come up with something far more dark and exotic to explain it.

But they couldn't have made up *everything*, could they? The playboy lifestyle? The dangerous reputation? It had been fifteen years since she'd last seen him so of course he wasn't going to be the same boy she'd known. As Katie gabbled on, Archie let her head drop back, the cool concrete of the pillar seeping into her brain, and tried to think a little more clearly. Maybe opening the Kaspar Athari can of worms really wasn't the best idea she'd ever had.

As Katie's hands grabbed her shoulders and hauled her off the pillar, Archie was tugged back to the present.

'This is your chance, here comes your Surgeon Prince.'

Before she could stop it, she was being swung around and thrust out around the column. The breath whooshed from her body. She didn't need to turn to know that Katie would have already gone.

'And there I was thinking you were hiding from me, Archie.'

The rich, slow drawl was laced with a kind of lazy amusement as every inch of Archie's skin prickled and got goosebumps. Not least the fact that he knew who she was after all. Her stomach spiralled like a helter-skelter in reverse.

Archie. He rolled her name on his tongue as though sampling it, tasting it. She imagined he was measuring it against the woman she was now, compared to the 'Little Ant' he'd always known her as.

She opened her mouth to speak just as Kaspar stepped closer to her. Everything in her head shut down as her body shifted into overdrive. Heady, and electrifying, and like nothing she'd ever known before.

He was dressed smart-casual, a vaguely lemony, leathery scent toying with her nostrils, and he practically *oozed* masculinity. Enough to eclipse every other male in the room most probably. Even every other male in the county. The world.

Even her childhood crush on him didn't compare. It made her feel physically winded and adrenalin-pumped all at once.

The indolent crook of his mouth, so sinful and enticing, gave the distinct impression that he could read her thoughts. Feed into her darkest desires. It made her very blood seem to slow in her veins. A sluggish trickle, which her thundering heart seemed to be working harder and harder to process.

He was simply intoxicating. She cast around for something, anything, that wouldn't betray how at sea she felt.

'How is the patient? Rick, wasn't it?'

Not exactly ideal, but it would have to do. Kaspar only hesitated for a moment.

'He's in pretty bad shape.'

'But you can help him?'

'Possibly.'

He didn't want to talk shop, she could understand that, but it was buying her some much-needed time. She had to settle down. Katie was right, she was like a beachgoer on hot sand.

'I think I read last year that you had a patient who'd had a firework go off in his face and you used some kind of layering technique?'

'You're in the medical profession?' Kaspar's stare intensified.

Archie swallowed. Hard.

'No, actually I'm in the construction industry. I build the hospitals, you work in them.'

'You build them?'

'Well, I work out layout, ease of movement so it isn't a rabbit warren; service routes such as for heating, lighting and medical gases especially for the operating rooms; whether to connect to the existing back-up generators, or build new ones; medical incinerators, that sort of thing.'

There was a lot more to it, and given how much she loved her job she could probably go on about it all night. Which would be a problem. It was hardly the most seductive of conversations.

'Are you part of the team building the new women's and children's wing for our hospital?'

Pride outweighed her need to change the subject.

'Yes.'

'I'm impressed. It's looking really good and I believe you're pretty much on time and on budget.'

She was powerless to prevent a grin so wide it might well crack her face in two.

'Thanks. It isn't going too badly. There are a few niggles but I built decent float into the programme so it shouldn't be too much of an issue. Once we've finished on the new wing we'll start on the new hospice facility across the site. We should be done within ten months, hopefully.'

'Even more impressive.'

'Dad always loved what I did,' she added suddenly.

Waiting, *hoping*, for Kaspar to add something he also remembered about her father. Then fighting the sense of discouragement when he barely even reacted.

'I can imagine.'

'Anyway,' she caught herself, 'we were talking about your firework patient.'

She didn't know why it felt so important that he should answer her. Perhaps because her dad had once told her and Robbie that getting Kaspar to open up about the things he loved was the key to knowing the boy. He kept everything that mattered to him so closely guarded, as though he feared the pleasure could be snatched from him at any time. The way his mother had often cruelly snatched away anything he'd shown an interest in as a kid, from toys, to hobbies, to his only decent stepfather.

According to her dad, Kaspar had never been a kid in the strictest sense of the word. His parents' volatile relationship had caused him to grow up quickly, to distance himself from people, to distrust easily. But her own father had brought him round, treating him exactly as he'd treated Robbie, encouraging when he could, laying down the ground rules at other times. And she'd treated him like a brother while Robbie, of course, had just been Robbie, sweet, funny and easygoing.

Did Kaspar remember all that? If he did, did he care? Enough to answer her?

He hesitated and, for a moment, she thought he was going to sidestep it.

'The boy's jaw was shattered. He'd lost a

chunk of it along with the teeth on the right side. He couldn't eat, couldn't even speak, so I needed to build a new jaw and simultaneously implant teeth. We layered pieces of titanium and then used a laser to harden the material. The lattice structure allowed us to really bend and form it so that it was the right size and shape for the kid, fitting perfectly and looking natural.'

Archie didn't realise she'd been holding her breath until he stopped speaking. He was looking directly at her, his eyes were dark, intense, like a moment of understanding. Of connection.

She didn't know whether it was a good or a bad thing that at that moment the music cranked up a notch and whatever else he was saying was lost, swallowed up by the thumping bass line.

'Say that again?' she shouted, but he shook his head.

The moment of opening up to her about his career was clearly over. She leaned in to speak into his ear, swaying slightly on her friend's heels, her body lurching against his as he put his arm around her to steady her. Her lips grazed his skin and she smelled the tantalising citrus scent.

It hit her again, that wall of primal need, stealing her breath away as his touch seared every inch of her flesh. It was almost a relief when the music kicked down again and he released her.

'You want to get out of here?' she asked instead.

'Together?'

'Is that a problem?'

The words were out before she had even thought about them. Seductive, teasing, another flash of the old, adult Archie. Yet the way she could never have dreamed of being as a thirteen-year-old with a crush. It was exhilarating.

'Not for me,' he growled. 'But, then, I'm sure you've heard the endless scandals that seem synonymous with my name. This isn't a high-profile charity event, but it isn't a small gathering either. If any press spot us, your photo will be on the internet before we even get to my hotel.'

'Is that your attempt to warn me?' She deliberately rolled her eyes. 'Only I make it a point never to believe idle gossip. I don't think they know the old Kaspar.'

'The *old* Kaspar?' His brow furrowed and as two light indentations peeked out from between his eyebrows a wave of familiarity unexpectedly coursed through Archie, making her clench her fingers into a fist just to keep from reaching out and lightly skimming them even as her stomach executed another downward dive.

So he *didn't* know who she was. No wonder he hadn't reacted to her mention of her father. Sick disappointment welled in her, but instead of backing away, as she might have done, a flash of the daredevil Archie Katie had been talking about suddenly flared within her.

Maybe, just maybe she could jog his cobwebbed memory. She would rather he piece it together himself than simply hit him over the head with it. She didn't want to risk anything that might make him back away from her.

'You know, the pre-"Surgeon Prince of Persia" reputation,' she prompted. 'The kid who climbed trees, and built dens, and fought with his best friend.'

Another beat. Imperceptible to perhaps anyone else. She felt rather than saw the shift.

'There is no pre-"Surgeon Prince of Persia".' He winked.

It should have irritated her, being altogether too seductive, suggestive and downright over-confident. It didn't. She'd seen the façade sliding back into place as though he regretted his moment of perceived weakness. That *tell* she recognised from long ago. More polished now, but there nonetheless. Kaspar the playboy might be standing in front of her, but she'd seen the Kaspar she'd known, the one she'd wanted, was still in there. She could still unearth him. For a moment back there she had succeeded.

A thrill coursed its way through her, lending her the confidence she'd been lacking.

'I don't know whether to admire your confidence or deplore your arrogance.' She cocked her head to one side as if genuinely giving it serious consideration. 'I rather fear it's the latter.'

'Oh, I seriously doubt that.'

His wolfish smile did little to soothe her jangling nerves. It was as though he was enjoying the banter. Relishing the challenge. Maybe if she dropped the right prompts, he would finally realise who she was. Finally remember.

'Are you really the blasé Lothario the press paint you as? Bedding a different woman every other night?' she challenged.

'Well, if it's in the press, then it must be true.'

Which wasn't really, she couldn't help but notice, an answer at all. It begged the question of why, if he was more like the Kaspar she remembered than the Kaspar the media seemed to describe, he would ever have allowed this unfavourable reputation of his to slide?

'So you haven't slept with any of the hundreds of women you've been linked with over the years?'

'I didn't say that either.' His teeth almost gleamed and Archie shivered as she felt their sharp edges as surely as if he had them against her skin.

Grazing her. Nipping her. An intimacy she'd read in books or experienced in her fantasies. Never in real life. Certainly not with Joe. She held his gaze, steady and sure, until eventually—incredibly—he broke his gaze.

Archie wasn't sure who was more surprised, her or Kaspar himself.

'I confess that I'm always impressed how I have the time to date quite so many women. Although I won't deny that when I get chance I do enjoy the company of the fairer sex.'

Something kicked hard, low in her stomach.

'Of course you do.'

'I am, after all, a man.' He took a step closer

to her and she found herself backing up to the pillar, her entire body fizzing with anticipation. 'Or are you going to pretend that you haven't noticed?'

'And if I said I hadn't?'

'I'd say that, public perceptions and exaggerations aside, I know women well enough to read that such an assertion would be a lie.'

'Is that so?' She barely recognised the husky voice coming out of her mouth. And Kaspar only cranked that sinful smile up all the higher.

'That's so. You noticed me. What's more, you want me. Almost as much as I want you.'

'There's that hubris again.'

'Perhaps it is hubris.' He took another step closer, not looking remotely remorseful. 'But it doesn't make it any less true. Shall we put it to the test?'

Suddenly, she was caged. The pillar at her back and Kaspar on the other three sides. Huge, and powerful, and heady. He wasn't actually touching her, and yet she felt the weight of him pressing in on her. Holding her immobile.

Not that she felt remotely like trying to escape.

'You really are altogether too sure of yourself.' She had no idea how she managed to sound so breezy.

Especially considering the frenzy into which her body currently seemed hell-bent on working itself. Lust and longing stabbed through her.

'Imagine how disappointing it would be if you fell short.'

He actually looked affronted just for a split second, before his eyes crinkled and a warm laugh escaped his lips. It was as though all the air in the room—in the world—went into that laugh. As though she didn't need it to breathe and could exist on that laugh alone. As though there was nothing else but Kaspar.

'I can assure you, Archie, I do not...*fall short*. In any respect.'

Her name on his lips again. If only she had the guts to reach up and kiss him, to discover whether his mouth tasted just as good as she imagined. She tried to but her body wouldn't move, probably due to this overriding need for him to recognise her properly. So in the end she simply stared back into eyes, which were all too familiar. In colour if not in expression.

'Well, of course, you would think that.'

'It isn't a matter of what I think.' His dark,

indolent tone spiralled through her. Every inch of her body felt it wrapping around her. Pulling tighter. Drawing her closer. 'It's a matter of what I know.'

It was all she could do to offer a nonchalant eye-roll.

'Let me guess. A hundred women hailing you as a deity in the throes of passion?'

She didn't want to think of those stories the papers loved to run with. The fact that his sexual prowess was lauded quite as much by quite so many. Although, now he'd mentioned it, it didn't add up that he should be quite such a driven, dedicated surgeon and yet have so much time for personal indulgences.

'Bit of an exaggeration. Although, frankly, I wasn't thinking of a single other woman. I was only interested in one. And she's standing right in front of me.'

'Oh, you *are* good,' she conceded, hoping against hope she didn't look half as flushed as she felt.

Hoping he couldn't hear the drumming of her heart or the roaring of blood in her ears. Hoping he couldn't read the lust pouring through her and making her nipples ache they were so tight. Hoping he couldn't feel the heavy heat pooling at the apex of her legs the way no man had ever made her feel before. At least not quite so wantonly.

She had a terrible fear that perhaps no other man would make her feel that ever again.

'Care to confirm that conclusion?' he murmured, his voice pouring over her just the way she would imagine warm, melted chocolate would do.

If she'd ever been that sexually adventurous, of course. Which she never had been. She imagined this version of Kaspar was, though, and the thought made her pulse leap in her wrists, at her throat.

What was the matter with her?

Kaspar didn't miss a thing. His eyes dropped to watch the accelerated beat, his face so close she could almost draw her breath as he exhaled his. His eyes never left hers, their intentions unmistakeable.

What wouldn't she have given for Kaspar to look at her like this when they'd been kids and she'd been besotted with him? And now he was.

Before she could stop herself, she reached out to trace the scar Katie had mentioned earlier.

'Is this really the result of some drunken bar brawl?'

'What else could it be?' His voice rasped over her as though his very fingers were inching down her spine. It was all she could do not to give in to a delicious shiver.

'I don't know, something more banal.' Archie had no idea how she managed to execute such an atypically graceful and nonchalant shrug. 'Like a childhood accident. Falling off a bike? Charging into a table? Tumbling from a tree?'

His eyes sharpened for a moment.

Something hanging there. Teetering between them.

'You have brothers?'

Her breath caught in her chest. A tight ball of air. Was Kaspar finally remembering?

A slew of emotions rushed her. Feelings she'd thought long since dead and buried. Idealistic, romantic, intense fantasies she'd cherished as an adolescent fancying herself in love with the oblivious Kaspar.

He'd ruined her, without ever touching her. Archie was sure of it. His mother had hauled him back to America right at the peak of her crush on him. If that hadn't happened, no doubt the infatuation would have run its course, as it did with most young girls. Instead, for years, she'd imagined she and Kaspar to be some kind of modern-day star-crossed Romeo and Juliet, torn away from each other before Kaspar had even had a chance to open his eyes and see what had been in front of him all along. She'd carried the ridiculous dream with her long after she should have let it die.

It was the reason she'd never had a serious boyfriend, always holding a part of herself back in her relationships. Until Joe, of course. But that had been tainted with other issues.

Now, suddenly, she had the chance to be with Kaspar. Only for one night, perhaps, but why not? They were both adults. She might never have imagined herself having a one-night stand before—she probably wouldn't with anyone else in the world—but Kaspar wasn't just anybody. Forget the wicked playboy everyone else knew. She wanted one night with the first and only boy she'd ever had a crush on. It might not be who Kaspar was any more, but at least it would help her to finally let go of her unrealistic, romantic, adolescent ideals.

Too late, she realised that his last words hadn't been a question as he'd pieced together who she was but more about explaining her accuracy away as if she was any girl with a brother.

'Nice guess. Most boys have fallen out of tree at one time or another,' he muttered. 'Still, it's refreshing to meet someone who would prefer to see the good in someone rather than simply believe all the media scandal.'

'No one can be quite as two-dimensional as the press seem to like to paint your Surgeon Prince alter-ego,' she breathed, willing the shutters to stop rolling down over his eyes.

'You'd think,' he offered flatly. 'But they're right about me. The bar brawl, the women, the flashy lifestyle. All things a girl like you would be best staying away from.'

It was impossible not to bristle, even as her entire body lamented the way he was pulling back from her.

'I'm twenty-eight, hardly a mere *girl*.'

'But too nice to get chewed up and spat out by the press, which, I can assure you, would happen if I kissed you the way I want to.'

It purred through her, starting at her toes and gaining speed and strength, until by the time it reached her head the roar was so loud in her ears that Archie was almost shocked the entire party couldn't hear it.

He wanted to kiss her. *Kaspar* wanted *her.*

'Let me get this straight.' She had no idea how her vocal cords even remembered how to speak. 'On one hand the infamous playboy Kaspar Athari is telling me that he lives up to his depraved reputation and on the other he's trying to protect mine by not sleeping with me?'

'Call it a Christmas miracle.'

'You're quite a few months out,' she pointed out shakily. 'What *would* people say if I told them you weren't quite the bad boy they think you are?'

'They wouldn't believe you,' he answered simply.

It felt like a sad fact.

Worse was the fact that he was pulling away from her. Ironic that she'd been right about him being the old, good Kaspar deep down, and that it was exactly *that* Kaspar who was trying to protect her now. Even though he still didn't recognise her.

She couldn't let that happen.

She couldn't allow this one opportunity to slip away from her because she'd let the last few years beat her down. She'd promised Katie she was getting back to her old self. She'd sworn to herself on that skydive that it was the moment she finally stepped away from the mess of the last five years or so.

If she wanted Kaspar, she was going to have to prove it. And she was going to have to tell him who she really was.

Leaning forward before she could second-guess herself, Archie fitted her mouth to Kaspar's. And she kissed him.

CHAPTER FOUR

IT WAS ONE of the most extreme, adrenalin-fuelled rushes of Kaspar's life. Like nothing he'd experienced before. Ever.

And it was only a kiss.

What would it be like to touch every millimetre of her? Taste her? Bury himself inside her? He'd never wanted a woman with such fierce intensity. Fighting the need to possess her with his body in exactly the way he was now possessing her with his mouth. Claiming her and stamping her as his.

He angled his head, the fit becoming tighter, snugger, and when his tongue scraped against hers, she answered it so perfectly that he felt it through every inch of his being. Her body surged against his as though she couldn't get close enough and her arms looped around his neck as though she couldn't trust her legs to stand up on their own.

Kaspar wasn't sure that his own could.

What was it about this woman?

A few minutes ago he'd been priding him-self—not to mention surprising himself—on the urge to protect her by staying the hell away from her. Then she'd kissed him and he'd lost the tight sense of self-control he'd honed to perfection over the last fifteen years. Despite what the press said about him.

The urge to press her to the pillar and shut out the rest of the partygoers was almost over-whelming. But if he did that, he was afraid he would lose himself completely. Here, in a dark corner of a club. He couldn't even think straight. He would never know how he found the strength to pull away.

She looked startled, then embarrassed, but before he could say anything she was already pulling herself together.

'Tell me that wasn't all you've got?' Teasing him again. But he didn't miss the undertone, the hint of uncertainty.

Somehow it only made him want her more.

Ignoring the alarm bells going off in his head, Kaspar forced himself to step away from her. The sense of loss was as shocking as it was nonsensical. He placed his hand at her elbow, telling himself it was only to guide her away from their current position, but he knew that wasn't entirely true. It was an excuse to touch her again.

'You mentioned getting out of here?' he muttered. A statement disguised as a question.

'Yes. *Hell, yes.*' She started forward, then stopped abruptly and placed her hand on his chest, the shake of her fingers betraying how much effort it was taking her. 'Before we do, there's something I need to tell you.'

Kaspar fought the bizarre urge to throw her over his shoulder and carry her out.

'Can it wait?'

Talking was pretty much the last thing on his mind right now.

'I guess.'

He couldn't decipher her expression. Guilt? Or relief?

In that instant, it didn't matter to him. His fingers closed around hers and he couldn't seem to lead her away fast enough. Anticipation made him feel drunk even though he hadn't touched a drop all night—rarely did, despite what the press loved to report—but no alcohol had ever made him feel like this. Like Archie made him feel. He made a brief call to his chauffeur to bring the car around. He just wanted to be alone with her. He *needed* to be, like the hormone-ravaged teen he'd never been.

Ducking down the stairs and past the few photographers milling around was easier than he'd expected, and his car was waiting right outside the door, Still, it was all he could do not to bundle her inside.

'Mine or yours?' he asked, wanting her to feel in control.

'Mine.' She didn't hesitate. 'I don't want to run another gauntlet of photographers.'

She probably wouldn't, but he didn't intend to argue.

'Come here.' His voice was raw, aching.

Obediently, she shuffled across the back seat towards him, having given the driver her address, but he could see her mind still whirring, and knew she was going to try that *talking* stuff again. It was a complication he could do without. Scooping her up, he hauled her into the air before settling her on his lap. His body tautened with approval.

'Much better.'

'Much,' she managed.

And then his mouth was claiming hers again, his hands roaming her body as she straddled him, the way he'd so urgently wanted to do in the club. From the exquisite curve of her calves to toy at the back of her knees, and then up those impossibly long thighs. But instead of going higher, he toyed with the hem of her short dress, then traced a path up her body instead, over the top of the metallic tassels. The material remained a barrier between them, the halter neck almost taunting him as it concealed her breasts from his gaze.

He cupped her chin with one hand, allowing the other to slide into her mass of blonde hair and cradle the back of her head. And for her part Archie met him stroke for stroke, making an exploratory journey of her own over his shoulders, his arms, his torso. She traced every curve and muscle and sinew, and let her head fall back as he scorched a trail of kisses from her mouth, down the elegant line of her neck and to the hollow by her clavicle. Her intoxicating scent filled his nostrils and heightened his senses.

With every sweep of her tongue and graze of her nails, she was driving him wilder and wilder. The fact that her fingers trembled as they undid the buttons of his dress shirt only added to the delicious tension. He yearned to know every inch of her. Intimately and completely. Reaching up, he unhooked the clasp at the back of her neck and allowed the two sides to fall down, exposing the most incredible breasts and hard, pinkish-brown nipples, which seemed to call out to him.

Kaspar couldn't resist. He bent his head and took one perfect bud in his mouth, his tongue swirling around it before he tugged on it. Just the right side of rough.

Her sharp gasp was like a caress against the hottest, hardest part of him. And then she offered the other breast for the same and as he obliged he couldn't stop a groan of desire slipping from his lips. He liked this bold, demanding side of her. He didn't know why, but he got the impression it wasn't a side of her that everyone got to see.

The idea appealed to him far more than it should have.

Lifting his hand, Kaspar lavished attention on one breast as he lowered his mouth to the other. Sucking on the nipple and then drawing back to watch her shiver as the cool air did the rest. He tried it again. And then again as he swapped sides. Until she wriggled on his lap, unmistakeable heat against the most sensitive part of his body. He reacted. Already hard, he was now so solid it was almost painful. Aching to touch her wet heat, to slide inside her.

But not here. Not in the car. With anyone else maybe he wouldn't have cared, but no one else had ever turned him on with quite the feverish quality that Archie had. He only knew he wanted more with her, and not on the back seat of a car.

'What's wrong?' she asked, sensing his change of attitude immediately.

Moving his hands to her hips, Kaspar shifted her backwards slightly. Enough so that every tiny movement of her hips didn't make his body throb quite so tightly.

It damn near killed him.

'Not here. Not the first time,' he managed hoarsely.

'The first time?' She arched one eyebrow as though that would distract him from the way her body quivered on his lap. Her pent-up tension equal to his. 'You're optimistic.'

'Once isn't going to be enough,' he bit out, the rawness in his own voice catching even himself by surprise. When had *that* become a fact? 'You must know that.'

The distinct hitch of her breath didn't help.

But whatever answer she might or might not have been about to give was cut short when the driver pressed the intercom to let them know they'd arrived, moments before the car pulled up.

He could barely believe the ridiculous way he couldn't seem to think straight with this woman. She made him lose his head.

Worse, a part of him *liked* it.

Archie opened the door to her apartment and reached for the lights.

Her skin still sizzled at the mere memory of his touch. It was impossible to shake the presentiment that she would never again be able to quash this shiver that ran so deep inside her. She had absolutely no idea how she managed to keep her voice so calm.

'So here we are.' She licked her lips anxiously. This was the first time she'd ever had a man back to *her* home. In fact, this was the first home she'd ever had by herself. 'In my apartment.'

Kaspar looked around.

'Nice place. Been here long?'

She shifted her weight from one leg to the other. This was her chance to tell him.

'Ten months. Since my marriage fell apart.' She shrugged, as though it hadn't felt like yet another catastrophic failure on her part, in her litany of mistakes over the last five years.

'You were married?' He made no attempt to hide his shock.

'For almost four years.'

'What happened?'

'I thought I loved him. I thought he loved me.' Another shrug as she desperately tried to keep the evening light. 'In hindsight, we rushed into it. My father had just died and my brother had emigrated. I was looking for something to fill a void, and Joe was it. He was kind and he cared for me. It was a mistake.'

She couldn't tell him about Faith. She wouldn't be able to dismiss that loss as lightly. Besides, he was still processing the bombshell she had just dropped.

But what choice had she had? He'd rebuffed her attempts to talk to him. To tell him.

'Your father had died, and your brother had emigrated?'

He raked his hand through his hair. A nostalgia-inducing young-boy action she hadn't seen in any press photograph of him for years. Perhaps ever.

She swallowed, her tongue feeling too thick for her shrinking mouth. Then she raised a shaking hand to a small cluster of photos on the wall. They could say all the things she couldn't.

He peered at them. Stepped closer. Stared harder.

She imagined she could see his eyes moving from one to the other. Photos of Robbie, of her father, of herself. And even the one with Kaspar himself.

The growing look of shock on his face twisted in her gut. He honestly hadn't had any idea. The knowledge clawed at her insides. The silence crowded in on them. Sucking every bit of air from the room, making it impossible for her to breathe. It was an eternity before Kaspar spoke, the words hissing out of his mouth like some kind of accusation.

'Little Ant?'

Despite his incredulity there was also a tenderness in the way he said her old nickname that pulled at her in a way she hadn't been prepared for. And he'd addressed her as an individual in her own right, not simply as *Robbie's sister*, which had to mean something, didn't it?

Even so, he was already physically backing away, heading towards the door. And she hated it. Now, more than ever, she wanted that connection with him. The moment they had never had.

Abruptly, desperation lent her an outward strength. Her voice carried an easy quality that she hadn't felt for years, even though her internal organs were working as hard as if they were completing some marathon or other.

'It's Archie now,' she offered redundantly. Awkwardly.

'God! I kissed you.'

Whether he was more disgusted at himself or at the kiss, she couldn't be sure. Either way, it was everything she'd feared.

'We kissed each other,' she corrected, madly trying to slow her thundering pulse. 'Oh, don't tell me you're suddenly getting all funny about it.'

'Of course I am,' he snarled, his eyes glittering. Dark, and hard, and cold...and something else. Something she couldn't identify. 'You used to be the closest thing to a little sister.'

He headed for the door, unable to sound more disgusted if he'd tried.

'Exactly. *Used* to be,' Archie echoed, refusing to cow at his tone, however it might claw at her. 'It has been fifteen years, Kaspar, and you didn't even recognise me. To all intents and purposes I'm no different from many other women at that party.'

'You aren't any other woman at that party. You're Little Ant. You're far more innocent than any of them.' He reached for the door, opened it, and she'd never felt more powerless. 'Certainly for someone like me. I have to get out of here. Now.'

And suddenly everything slowed down for Archie. She could read the anger and anguish at war on his face, and she realised what was going on. It bolstered her. A rush of confidence warmed her.

'You're not angry with me for not telling you so much as being angry at yourself that you still want me.' Her voice held wonder. 'You *really* want me.'

He didn't stop, didn't even falter. He just continued walking right out of the door.

'I'm exactly the kind of guy you should stay away from, Little Ant.'

'I'm not Little Ant, Kaspar. I haven't been that girl for over ten years. I'm a woman now, with a career, and my own home, and a failed marriage.'

He hesitated in the hallway, just as she'd

hoped he would, and turned to face her. He was still fighting temptation, she could tell, but he knew his arguments were holding less and less sway. Deliberately she swept her tongue over her lips, as if to wet them.

His eyes slid down and watched the movement with a darkening expression. A thrill coursed through her. He wanted to do what he thought was the morally right thing, he was *trying* to do it. But things had gone too far in the car. They'd been too intimate. And now he was having a difficult time turning the attraction off just like that.

'I thought you were in Australia.'

He was stalling, she realised incredulously. No one would ever believe it. Not the press, not the public, certainly not the broken-hearted women who flailed in his wake.

'Robbie went after Dad died because his then girlfriend, now wife, was from there. My life was here. I'd just finished my degree, I had a new job…'

'You'd met your husband.'

She couldn't place the edge to his tone, but she did know the moment she'd been imagining was slipping away from her. Too fast.

She needed to salvage the evening, convince

Kaspar that she wasn't that kid any more. She was the woman he'd been kissing, holding, touching in the car.

'As nice as this little catch-up might be, we didn't come back here to my flat to shoot the breeze, did we, Kaspar?'

She couldn't decide whether he admired her forthrightness, or if it merely caught him off guard. Either way, she didn't care. She had a small window in which to press her advantage. If she missed it, that would be it.

She stepped forward boldly and flashed him a cheeky grin, disarming him.

'Good, so now we've aired our concerns, can we get back to the fun we were having in the car?'

'Archie, are you listening to me?' he bit out, but he didn't move away.

She stepped forward again.

'I'm trying not to. It's hardly the greatest foreplay conversation. Certainly not worthy of the great Surgeon Prince of Persia.'

'This isn't going to happen,' he warned, his voice gritty. Not entirely as forceful as she imagined he could be.

'I'm pretty sure it already has. Or have you

forgotten just how intimate we were on the car journey here?'

She heard the low growl, which reverberated around her. She knew the image of his mouth on her nipples, making her moan and writhe on his knee, was as imprinted in his head as it was in hers. He was close to giving in to her. To this attraction. She just needed to give him that nudge over the edge.

'I'm leaving now, Archie.' He reached his hand out to grab the door handle and close the door behind him.

She had one last chance to stop him.

'Are you sure?' she asked evenly, even as she reached up to the back of her neck, undid the clasp and let the dress drop to the floor, past the flimsy scrap of electric-blue lace, to pool around the skyscraper heels, which she suddenly didn't remotely feel silly wearing.

She felt sexy and powerful and wicked.

But Kaspar wasn't moving. And she had absolutely no idea what he was thinking.

He couldn't move.

Frozen to the spot, his eyes riveted to the vision in front of him, for the first time in his life

Kaspar felt powerless. He should leave. Turn around and walk away. But he couldn't bear to.

She was sublime. So completely and utterly perfect. The tasselled Latin-dance-style dress might have looked good on her, but they hadn't flattered the sexy, voluptuous curves of her body anywhere near as generously as they should have. They should have worshipped her...the way he ached to do right at this moment.

The pictures were still on the wall, a mere few feet away, but he couldn't reconcile the kid in those photos with the woman standing in front him. This one was a *siren*.

From the long line of her neck, down to glorious breasts, which he hungered to cup, caress, kiss, down to the indent of her waist and the belly button around which he could imagine swirling patterns with his tongue. His eyes dropped lower, appreciative and unhurried, to take in the soft swell of her belly and the sensational flare of her hips, and then the incredible V of her legs where the scrap of blue lace, barely concealing her modesty, only seemed all the more titillating.

'Tell me you don't want me, Kasper,' she murmured. The faintest hint of a quiver in her voice, a moment of uncertainty, only making her all the more irresistible.

His entire body pulled taut. Unequivocal male approbation. God, how he wanted to be where that lace was. With his fingers, his mouth, his sex. He couldn't recall ever having ached to be with a woman before. Not like this.

'You know I want you,' he rasped, unable to keep the admission from spilling from his lips.

'Then claim me,' she breathed, offering herself to him.

But now it was about more than just sex. Perhaps it always had been. Perhaps a part of him had known he knew her, even if he hadn't recognised her. It certainly explained the connection he felt.

And that in itself posed the greatest threat. Archie knew him in a way no one else did. Not the press, and not his previous lovers. And that made her dangerous. Hadn't she already told him that she knew the playboy image wasn't really him?

She saw too much. She knew him too well. And that enabled her to slip under his skin every time he wasn't paying full attention. He certainly couldn't afford to spend the night with her.

He hadn't turned himself into the press's idea of the Surgeon Prince of Persia because he'd wanted to be a playboy. He'd turned himself into that two-dimensional version of himself because, ultimately, it was all he deserved. Because his bad-boy image was the only thing that stopped them painting him out as some kind of surgeon hero. And he wasn't a hero.

Just ask the family of that kid whose life he'd changed that night in the bar. But the press had never run with that story. They, like the judge, had vindicated him, Kaspar, of all blame. No matter that he had been the one able to walk out of the hospital that night while the other kid hadn't.

It was why he'd deserved his bad-boy reputation all these years. It was why Archie should stay away from him. And it was why he should walk out of her door now.

But, then, who in their right mind could walk away from someone like her?

Not just because she looked quite like... *that*. But because there was something more than just the physical, more than the undeniable sexual attraction that crackled between them. There was a connection. He'd felt it on the plane, although it had taken him until now to recognise it for what it was.

Archie knew him in a way that no one else did.

Despite the media's potted history of his less-than-enviable childhood, pushed and pulled between two parents who had seen him more as a pawn in their sick game than as a flesh-and-blood boy who either of them loved or wanted, it had nevertheless always been somewhat sanitised and glamorised. Entertainment channels ran specials on his actress mother and himself but they had never, ever even come close to how miserable it had actually been.

In many ways he was grateful for that. But Archie wouldn't be fooled by it. Her father had been the one to save him. She had been there through enough of his childhood to know the truth. Not all of it. No one but him knew all of it. But certainly closer to the truth than anyone else ever could. Or would.

And that was the problem.

He allowed people to paint him as the cad, the womaniser, because that ensured that no one really knew him, understood him, could get close to him. And if they couldn't do that then they couldn't get under his skin. He couldn't bear the idea that anyone could break through his mental armour and make him feel…something…*anything* because then he'd have to feel all those terrible childhood emotions all over again.

It wasn't just that he was a danger to Archie… she was a danger to *him*. To his sanity. And yet he still stood motionless. Powerless to resist her.

'Come and claim me, Kaspar,' she repeated, her voice cracking through the command.

He was sure it was the sexiest sound he'd ever heard.

Logic and sense flooded from his brain, something far more base and primal flooding the rest of his body.

'This can't lead anywhere, Archie. I fly back to the States next week. I don't know when I'll be back.'

'So you'd better make this the best night of your stay, hadn't you?'

So damn sassy. So damn sexy.

He heard the deep growl that seemed to come from the vicinity of his throat, was barely conscious of kicking the door closed behind him with an accurate jab of his foot, and found himself striding across the room towards her.

Towards Archie.

Some madness had taken hold of him, he was sure of it. And then Kaspar wasn't thinking of anything any more. He was dragging her into his arms, moulding her mouth-watering, practically naked body to his, and plundering her too temptingly carnal mouth. And his seductive siren wasn't remotely shy in her sudden state of undress.

Archie wound her arms around his neck, pressing herself so tightly against him he could almost imagine there wasn't a barrier of clothes between them at all, and lifted her legs to wrap around his body as he willingly cupped her firm, neat backside.

He kissed her mouth, her neck, every trembling inch of her collarbone, and she matched him. Kissing his jaw, tugging at his ear lobe and rocking her body against his sex until he feared he might not be able to hold on much longer.

'Which way?' he managed gruffly, scarcely ripping his mouth from hers.

Her reply wasn't much clearer.

'Behind me.'

Obligingly, Kaspar navigated his way to the door, shouldering it open and carrying Archie into the room, smiling at the queen-size bed with its overabundance of scatter cushions.

He lowered her down, less gently than he might have liked, holding himself still while she reached for the buttons on his shirt, undoing them with painstaking care, kissing her way over his chest and abdomen with each new section of bare flesh she exposed. It felt like an eternity before she finally undid the last button and he could shuck off the shirt, but it seemed Archie wasn't done. She reached for his belt, the crack of leather reverberating around the room as she unbuckled the clasp, followed by the unmistakeable sound of the zip opening.

Kaspar circled her wrist with his fingers and pulled away from her as she protested. He couldn't afford to let this go any further. He'd never felt such a lack of control, as if he might explode like a hormone-ravaged teenager. This was as much about Archie's pleasure as his.

He pressed her lightly back onto the bed and covered her body with his, bracing himself as he looked down at her, drinking her in. Marvelling. Every inch of his skin was on fire as Archie ran her fingertips over him, tracing the muscles on his shoulders and down his body.

Heady, and exhilarating, and addictive.

When he cupped her breast, his thumb grazing deliberately against one straining nipple, she gasped, her back arching slightly. Repeating it offered the same glorious result. Then Kaspar lowered his mouth and tasted her as he had in the car, his tongue tracing out an intricate whorl as Archie slid her fingers in his hair and gave herself over to pleasure. He took his time learning every last contour of her breasts, then her abdomen and her hips. Slowly. Thoroughly. Ignoring the almost painful, needy ache of his sex.

Finally, when her soft moans became more urgent, he laid a trail of hot kisses from her navel straight down over her belly and over the top of the flimsiest blue lace panties, which he pulled off in one swift movement. Then he dropped back down to press his mouth to the hottest, slickest, sweetest part of her, making her cry out.

She tasted of fire, and honey, and *need*. Her hips were moving, dancing with him, as he licked his way into her. Her hands cradled his head, the most beautiful, wanton sounds escaping her mouth almost against her will. It spoke to something utterly primal inside Kaspar. As if he would never get enough.

He kissed, licked, sucked until her hands slid from his hair to clutch the cover of the bed, her hips moving erratically, trying to jerk away.

'Please, Kaspar...' She reached for him, but despite the hunger in her voice he had no intention of taking his pleasure yet. This was about Archie.

'There's no rush,' he murmured. 'We've got all night.'

Then, slipping one hand underneath her to hold her in place, he lowered his mouth back down to her intoxicating heat and slid his finger inside her, deep and sure.

Archie shattered, crying out his name as she arched her back and fragmented all around him like some victory he couldn't identify. He kept it going long after she would have pulled away, making her shudder over and over, murmuring against her and making her come apart again.

And when she finally begged him to release her, he let her go, a satisfaction he couldn't explain seeping through to his very bones. As well as a slow, deep ache.

'That was...' She floundered for the words to describe the incredible way she felt. Like nothing she'd ever experienced before. Not even close. 'I feel... You were...'

'We're not done yet.'

His voice was gravelly, raw, and still it felt to Archie as though she was taking a lifetime to refocus. Her body felt exhausted, contented. She struggled to lift herself up onto her elbows.

'We aren't?'

'Not by a long stretch.'

She wasn't sure if it was an avowal or a warning, but the sight of Kaspar standing up, shedding himself of the rest of his clothes until he was naked before her, stole her breath away all over again. His solid physique and utterly male beauty, waiting there just for her, went beyond even her wildest fantasies. Archie let her eyes drop to take in his length, straight and flat against his lower abdomen, as taut and unyielding as a steel blade. Though she would have thought it impossible a moment before, her body gave a fresh kick of lust.

How could it be, after all that, that she wanted him again so instantly?

'That's a relief,' she tried to tease him, but the quake in her voice betrayed her. 'I was beginning to think that was all you had. After talking yourself up earlier tonight, I was expecting a lot more.'

'Is that so?' He arched one eyebrow and she couldn't contain the gurgle of laughter that rumbled in her chest.

'It was a…concern.'

Then he was moving back over her, nestling himself between her legs as his hands moved under her shoulders and he rested on his forearms above her.

'Then let me put your mind at ease. We have a long, long night ahead of us.'

Whatever witty response she might have come out with was chased from her head as he nudged against her hot, wet core. It was too much, and at the same time not enough. She sucked in a deep breath, her legs parting slightly further as his amused eyes caught hers.

'You were saying?'

She shook her head and bit her lip, unable to speak. And then he thrust into her. Hard and strong and deep, stretching her in a way that felt more delicious than uncomfortable. As though she'd been made for him; they'd been made for each other. She shifted instinctively and he groaned, making her feel sexy and powerful all over again. Archie watched him in fascination, his face pulled tight as though he was trying to control himself, as though *she* made him feel unrestrained.

She couldn't help it, this wanton side of her that seemed to be taking over tonight. Lifting her legs, she wrapped them around his waist, locking her heels at his back, drawing him even deeper into her slick, welcoming heat. He groaned again and it pulled at something low in her, and then his eyes caught hers, smoky and strong, the colour of richest brandy, his intent undisguised. Archie's breath hitched somewhere in her chest. All she could do was dig into his arms, his shoulders, as he began to move. A dance as old as time and a pace equally as steady. Her body was helpless to do anything but match it, stroke after stroke, thrust after thrust, his eyes never leaving hers.

She had no idea how long they moved together. A lifetime. Maybe longer. As though she had never been meant to be anywhere else but here. With Kaspar. Better than any of her dreams if only for the simple fact that this was real.

At some point he swept his hand down her side, her already sensitive body shivering at the feather-light touch, and then he was touching her at the centre of her need and there was nothing *feather-light* about it at all. He knew exactly what he was doing. And how much pressure he needed to exert.

Archie gasped and arched her back, her hips, her neck. She wanted to tell him to slow down, not because she didn't want this but because a tiny part of her couldn't stand the thought that he might leave as soon as this was all over, but her tongue refused to work. At least as far as talking was concerned. Instead, she slid her hands down his back, her nails leaving their own exquisite trail, and he shuddered and growled, plunging into her more deeply. So desperate and demanding and *right*. It threw her straight back over the cliff edge until she was tumbling and tumbling, and she didn't care where she landed so long as it was with Kaspar.

And as she called out his name, surrendering herself completely to him, this time Kaspar followed.

CHAPTER FIVE

'FOURTEEN HOURS OF surgery and it all comes down to this.' Kaspar grinned with satisfaction at his team. A reconstruction and rehabilitation procedure on a patient who had lost almost all of his upper jaw and teeth almost a decade earlier, following oral cancer surgery.

'Yeah, rebuilding a man's jaw and bone palate using advanced osteointegration and three-dimensional computerised design. It's awesome.'

Kaspar glanced at the young surgeon. Rich, arrogant, the son of a renowned surgeon, he came across entitled and lacking in empathy, but he was a solid surgeon, if only Kaspar could find a way to steer him.

'More than the medical kudos, it's going to be life-changing for our patient. He'd become almost hermit-like, unable to venture out without people pointing and staring.'

'I guess. But, still, we're, like, in ground-breaking territory here.'

Normally, today's surgery was exactly the kind of challenge on which Kaspar thrived. Had always thrived.

But despite his triumph, Kaspar was preoccupied. He had been ever since that stolen time with Archie almost five months ago.

Five months in which he hadn't been able to get her out of his head. The way she sounded, smelt, tasted. Night after night his body ached for her, in a way it never had for any other woman. He told himself it was just the sex, that he didn't recall the walks, the laughter, the shared memories with such clarity. He refused to admit to whatever alchemy went on in his hollow, astringent chest. Even so, one night hadn't been enough. He'd had to eke out the weekend, then an extra day. Even that hadn't sated the yearning he had for her.

Yearning.

Him.

Every day had been a battle not to contact her. Even whether or not to send her flowers when he'd seen the date a couple of months earlier and had realised it was her birthday. Every day he'd prayed for challenges like this one to walk into his consultation room, if only to have somewhere else to pin his focus.

But it always came back to Archie. And whether, if he took up the offer to return to the UK next month, he should contact her or not.

'I mean, think of it this way,' the younger man enthused, pulling Kaspar back to the present, 'using implant bone to live and grow around a titanium plate, being able to create the bone and tissue to support an implant of a whole new set of teeth. Traditionally we'd have had to use plates and grafts and cadavers.'

'And our patient,' Kaspar continued firmly. 'Being able to speak and be understood, or to eat food or have a drink without fluid spilling from his sinuses and mouth.'

But the young surgeon was only interested in the surgery, and Kaspar didn't have the inclination to lecture as he might otherwise have done. His head was too full of Archie.

He'd told himself he was too damaged. Too selfish. Too destructive. Especially for someone as bright and vibrant as Archie Coates was. He'd kept an ocean between them with the excuse that he was protecting her. But the truth was that he was concerned about her. The longer they'd spent together, the more he'd noticed that she'd seemed to have lost a little of the special lustre he remembered about her. As though life had somehow scratched at her when it shouldn't have. Her father's death, the idiot husband she'd mentioned, maybe even Robbie emigrating.

Whatever it was, something in him ached to be the one to take her pain away.

Ridiculous.

He was the last person to take *anyone's* pain away. It was better to keep his distance.

She was going to be sick.

Archie let her hand fall from the door for the third time in as many minutes, her legs threatening to collapse beneath her. Around six hours ago she'd still been somewhere across the Atlantic. And twelve hours before that she'd been to have a twenty-week ultrasound to determine that her baby was all right.

Their baby.

Hers and Kasper's.

She'd had months to get used to this but it had made little difference, it still felt utterly surreal to her. So how was it going to feel for Kaspar?

Perhaps she should have thought this through

better. Yesterday she'd only been grateful that her work and her life to date meant she had three years remaining on her visa which allowed her multiple visits to the States, for up to six months.

Foolishly, she'd taken it as some kind of sign.

The push she'd needed to go and find Kaspar. To tell him about their baby.

Now Archie stopped, one hand reaching out to lean on the wall, the other hand running tenderly over the slight swelling in her abdomen. It was incredible. A miracle. At least to her. Nothing would ever make up for losing her first baby, Faith, at eighteen weeks gestation, and no baby could ever replace her, but in some ways this new tiny human growing inside her went some way to healing those still-raw wounds.

She hovered outside the door, the small cabin bag and work laptop at her feet, trying to summon the courage to knock. It had to be the last thing he would want to hear. Might even prefer not to know. The Surgeon Prince of Persia a father? The press would have a field day.

Nevertheless, deep down she knew she owed it to this baby, and to herself, to at least tell him. To let him make that decision for herself.

Still, it was turning out to be a lot harder than she'd hoped it would be.

The old Archie would probably have blurted it out, however awkwardly or untimely. The Archie of the last few years might have shamefully buried her head for as long as she could.

But which Archie was she now? She was more confused than ever. Swinging wildly from the daredevil Archie of old, right over to the reticent woman of recent years, and then back again.

The skydive, then that night with Kaspar when she'd stripped—*stripped*—to seduce him, emboldened in a way she hadn't been for years. For weeks afterwards she'd strutted around feeling ten feet tall and even her friend, Katie, had been forced to admit Kaspar hadn't been such a bad influence after all.

When she'd discovered she was pregnant, it had been a moment of sheer joy and disbelief that her body had effortlessly achieved the one thing it had been struggling to do throughout her entire marriage to Joe. And then she'd been catapulted right back into the dark, cold prison of her mind.

The fear of losing this baby the way she'd lost Faith overrode everything else. With it, the uncertainty, the confusion, the regression to the hesitant Archie of the previous five years. And so she'd spent the past few months bouncing between the two polar opposite versions of herself.

It was how she'd had the confidence to fly halfway around the world to confront Kaspar, and yet now she was here she couldn't bring herself to lift her arm and knock on that door. She could make that final move or she could turn around, head straight back to the airport and be on a plane, with him none the wiser. The most shocking part about it was that Archie had absolutely no idea which way she was going to jump.

Who was she? Really?

And then the decision was taken out of her hands. The door suddenly opened and he was striding out. Stopping dead the instant he saw her.

'Archie.'

'Kaspar.'

There was a beat as his eyes seemed to take her in. Scanning her face, then dropping down. Another beat as they hovered around the evident swell of her belly.

Her whole world pinpointed around him, her

breath seeming to slow and then stop in her chest. Time had done little to diminish the impact he had on her. Maybe it had even amplified it. She had the oddest sensation of falling. Plummeting.

The question was, *How painful was the landing going to be?*

'You'd better come in,' he managed at last. The unusually hoarse tone to his voice only made her nerves jangle all the more.

Then he picked up her bags and was gone. Walking back into his office with as little surprise, as little emotion as if she'd been his next patient he'd been waiting to see.

Still, it took her several long moments before she was able to follow him.

She was barely through the door before he was speaking.

'You're pregnant.'

His voice seemed palpably colder now. More forbidding. Or perhaps it was just her nerves. Behind her the door closed with a soft *click*. It might as well have been the clang of prison gates but somehow it offered her the strength she needed.

'*Clearly* pregnant,' he added.

Had her hand wandered to the obvious swell

of her abdomen before or after his observation? Lifting her head, Archie met his eyes, not allowing her voice to falter for a second. Though how she managed it, she would never know.

'Yes.'

'We used protection,' he stated flatly.

A statement but not a defence. As though he didn't exactly disbelieve her. She was grateful for that much, at least. It allowed her to soften her voice somewhat.

'Not that first time.'

'So he or she really is mine?'

It felt like a slap across her face, although she supposed it was a reasonable enough question. Still, she couldn't seem to prise her jaws apart, answering him through gritted teeth.

'Who else's would it be, Kaspar? The invisible man's? I'm not in the habit of picking up random men or sleeping around. Yes, it's your baby. *Our* baby.'

It was impossible to follow the flurry of emotions that passed across his face. But, then, he had always been the poster-boy for denial. Pretending that he was happy, that his family life was fine, to his friends, his school, the world, when her family had seen first-hand how broken he'd been inside. How he'd spent every school holiday with them, along with his nanny, Maggie, just to avoid being dragged into yet another of his parents' twisted games against each other.

'He or she,' he bit out flatly.

'Sorry?'

'Say *he* or say *she*. Don't call the baby an *it*.'

She frowned, confused.

'I don't know whether it's a boy or a girl. I didn't find out. I didn't want to.'

'I don't care,' he growled, the unexpectedly menacing quality to his tone making her skin prickle. 'This baby is not an *it*. Pick *he* or *she*, interchange them, or I'll call her a *she* while you call him a *he*, for all I care. Just don't ever use the term *it* again.'

Fury swirled in his words, but it was the look of torment behind his eyes that really clutched at her, squeezing at her heart. A torment that made her wonder about the childhood she'd pieced together from things she remembered, things her father had said, things she'd read.

'Okay.' She dipped her head. 'I'll say *he*, you can say *she*.'

He didn't reply, but his lips curled in what she took to be a silent thank you.

'So you're...'

'Twenty weeks,' she cut in, barely able to help herself. Although he wouldn't have any idea how significant that was to her.

'You should have told me,' Kaspar bit out, and she had to protect herself against the kick of emotion. The irrational fear that by talking about it she was somehow jinxing things.

'Would you really have wanted to know?'

'That has nothing to do with it,' he almost snarled. 'You've had five months to tell me.'

He hadn't denied it. And even though she'd known the answer before she'd even asked the question, it still hurt.

But she couldn't let him see that. It took everything she had to keep her voice even.

'I'm telling you now.'

'That isn't good enough.'

'It will have to be.' She jutted her chin out, trying not to let him intimidate her.

He narrowed his eyes as if he could see straight through her. As if he knew there was something she was hiding.

'Why not?' he demanded abruptly.

Archie flinched.

'It's...irrelevant.'

'I don't believe that for a moment,' Kaspar barked, folding his arms across his chest.

She tried not to notice how it made his already wide shoulders seem all the bigger, his strong chest all the more unyielding. And she tried not to notice the long fingers that had done such...*things* to her. Over and over that night. That weekend.

When they'd made a baby.

What was she playing at? They were kids and this wasn't a game. She owed him an explanation.

'I didn't tell you because I was scared. I was pregnant once before.' She heard her voice crack but she pushed on, pretending it hadn't. A part of her had known this subject would come up. That it was inevitable. She was ready for it. 'Eighteen months ago. But I lost that baby at eighteen weeks.'

She stopped abruptly, pain ripping through her. Lacerating her from the inside out. Dizzying and unforgiving.

'I'm sorry,' he said simply.

'Her name was Faith.'

She didn't even realise she'd spoken until she heard the words. The agony that had haunted her ever since with *what ifs* and *if onlys*. The self-recriminations. She'd thought she'd been mentally prepared. She'd been dealing with the pain every single day, and each day it had felt just that tiny, minuscule bit easier. But hearing the words aloud, for the first time since it had happened...nothing could have prepared her for that.

She only realised he'd caught her from crumpling on the spot as she found herself in a seat she didn't recall moving to, and Kaspar coming back into the room, a steaming plastic cup in hand.

'Sweet tea.' He thrust it at her. 'Drink it. All of it.'

She didn't dare disobey.

Bit by bit, she sipped at the cup until it was empty. And Kaspar just sat opposite her. Waiting. Wordlessly. While the minutes ticked by. As if he had nowhere else to be but right here. With her.

Tears pricked her eyes and she blinked them back. She shouldn't read anything into that. It didn't mean anything. She couldn't afford to think it did.

'I...needed to get past that point...the eighteen weeks. And then I thought that when I had my twenty-week scan, if it...' What had they agreed, that she would call the baby *he*, and Kaspar would say *she*? 'If *he* was okay, I would tell you. So…here I am.'

She trailed off. Not quite sure how to articulate the storm that roiled around her entire body, constantly up-ending everything.

His eyes never moved from her. Clear and unblinking.

'So the scan was fine?'

'Yes. But these things are always fine until… until they're suddenly not.'

It was all she could do to keep her voice even and sound calm. There was no point in letting the dark fear that lurked deep inside her take a hold. No point in imagining scenarios that might never happen. The doctors didn't think there was anything they needed to worry about or do, so she had to trust them. They were the medical professionals. Not her.

'What are you doing?' She frowned as Kaspar stalked around his desk, snatched up the phone and stabbed a couple of numbers on the pad.

He didn't answer her, too intent on the call.

'Dr Jarvis, please, it's Dr Athari.' There was a brief pause. 'Catherine? It's Kaspar. I have a patient I need you to examine. It's urgent.

Archana Coates, twenty-nine-year-old, approximately twenty weeks pregnant.'

Too shocked to speak, Archie listened as he described her in completely dispassionate terms. Like a third person. *Like a patient.*

'She has a past history of spontaneous second-trimester abortion.' Archie flinched. It was the same terminology the doctors had used around her and she'd never hated a medical term so much in her life. It sounded so wrong, as if she'd had any choice in the matter whatsoever. Kaspar continued, oblivious. 'No, not a referral. It's personal.'

Within moments he had replaced the handset.

'What…what are you doing?'

'Catherine Jarvis is one of the best perinatologists in the world.' He paused as Archie stared at him in confusion, then clarified. 'Maternal-foetal specialist. She has a patient with her now but she'll see you in half an hour.'

'I don't… *No!*' Archie shook her head at the implications of what he was saying, the suggestion that the pregnancy wasn't as low-risk as she'd believed hitting her altogether too hard. 'I've had a scan. I've been checked. They know my history. If something was wrong, if it was going to happen again, they would have known.'

'Shh,' he soothed. 'I'm not saying they're wrong. I'm just… I want to be sure.'

But the expression in his eyes didn't exactly fit.

'Is the loss of the baby…of Faith why your marriage fell apart?'

She knew he was distracting her, but the very fact that he'd remembered her daughter's name cut through everything else. It was more than Joe had done. He hadn't even cared enough to want to name her.

'Yes,' she managed quietly. 'And no.'

'Meaning?' There was a slight curl to his lip, as though he couldn't help but sneer. As though he knew what kind a man Joe had been.

But he didn't know anything at all.

'He got the job opportunity of a lifetime in Switzerland. I didn't want to go with him.'

'Why not? He was your husband.'

'My life was in the UK, plus I'd just lost my baby, and I didn't love him,' she began hesitantly.

'You married a man you didn't love?' His censure made her bristle.

'I thought I loved him. I told him I loved

him. But, with hindsight, I don't know if I ever did or if I was more grateful to him. He was there after Dad died. I was falling apart and Joe looked after me. He was kind to me. He took care of me. He loved me. I thought I loved him, too.'

'Enough to marry him?' Kaspar didn't even try to keep the scorn from his voice.

'He was twelve years older than me. He was like a rock. Stable, emotionally secure, knew what he wanted, including a family. That all appealed to me. Now I know I was just trying to fill the void left by Dad's death and Robbie going to Australia.'

'It sounds like this bloke took advantage of you.'

'No.' She shook her head. 'At least, not like you're thinking.'

'He knew you were grieving and vulnerable and he seduced you into marriage by pretending to love you,' Kaspar accused.

'No, it wasn't like that.'

Archie shifted on her seat, splaying her hands out as though that could somehow help her articulate the words that were in her head but which she couldn't seem to get out.

'I think it was. You were lost and grieving

while he should have known better. I think when you finally see it for what it is, you'll stop making excuses for him.'

'I think the sooner you get your head out of your backside the sooner you'll stop trying to tell me exactly what I do or don't feel,' Archie snapped suddenly, taking both herself and Kaspar by surprise. A welcome flash of the vibrant, no-nonsense side of herself.

Still, she didn't expect Kaspar to drop his head back and let out a laugh.

'What's so funny?' she demanded coldly.

'You are. Welcome back, Little Ant.'

A small smile played on her lips, despite herself. He was right, and it felt good to see the re-emergence of her old feisty self.

Every time she was around him, it seemed.

Hastily, she bit her tongue before she could utter *that* particular nonsense aloud.

'I'm sorry for judging. For criticising.'

Kaspar's tone was surprisingly tender. Even…nostalgic? It elicited another smile from her, albeit this time a wry one.

'You and Robbie may have called me Little Ant, but Dad used to call me his Little Tardigrade.'

The throaty laugh rippled through her, doing

things to her it had no business doing. Rushing straight through her body and to her very core, where she was, shamefully, in danger of melting all over again.

'I think I remember that. You always were little but hardy.'

'Yet also, sometimes, more fragile than people thought,' she heard herself replying, too late to clamp down on her words, to swallow them back.

She'd never admitted that to anyone but her father before. Why on earth would she say it now? And to Kaspar, of all people.

'I never realised.' His face sharpened. Hard, angular lines that signified his disapproval. 'I always thought you were such a tough little thing. So strong.'

Archie took in his almost contemptuous expression. It left her feeling as though she'd let him down, let herself down, and she told herself that her heart wasn't being squeezed, right there, in her splintering chest. She gritted her teeth.

'Kaspar, I didn't come here to talk about my ex-husband or my historical mistakes. I just felt I owed it to you to tell you I was expecting a baby, *your* baby, and I didn't think it was something that I should do over the telephone.'

'And then what? You expected me to fall on one knee and propose? To play happy families?'

Actually, she hadn't thought past this awful meeting. But now he looked so dark, so forbidding, so cold, it was like being plunged into an icy, glacial milk flow. She got the sense that no amount of shivering would ever be able to warm her up while his eyes bored into her like this.

It occurred to her that her best form of defence right now was attack. She folded her arms, tilting her chin up and out as she forced herself to stare him down. Refusing to cower, however he might make her feel.

'No, Kaspar. I've been there, I've done that. Marriage isn't a mistake I intend to make again.'

'So then what? You thought you'd drop the bombshell and then hop on the next plane back to the UK?'

He was goading her, his scepticism unmistakeable. It was a struggle not to bristle. She had no idea how she forced herself to her feet.

Took her first few steps across the room as though she was in complete control of herself.

'I don't know what I expected you to do. Any more than, I suspect, you know what to do right now. But I just felt I owed it to you to at least tell you I was pregnant.' It was a hauteur she hadn't even known she possessed. 'Now that I have, I think it's time for me to leave.'

Kaspar, apparently, wasn't as impressed as she was.

'Sit back down, Archie,' he ground out furiously. 'You're mad if you think I'm letting you go anywhere with my baby.'

CHAPTER SIX

WHAT THE HELL was he playing at?

Pacing silently on the other side of the curtain as Catherine conducted a thorough examination of Archie, he struggled to quell the out-of-control fear that was spiralling inside him.

He wasn't ready to be a father. He'd never thought he ever would be. And that was another of the reasons why he'd always avoided romantic entanglements. He could never, ever risk being the kind of parent his father had been. Worse, being the kind of parent his mother had been. He remembered how it had felt to feel insignificant, unworthy, not...*enough.* Pain and grief poured through him, like the boilermakers he'd drunk as an unhappy, lost, late-teen; a shot of whisky chased down by a strong beer.

But now his life and Archie's were bound together. For ever. He'd known that after the first few moments of blind panic had cleared, back in his office. He would never allow a child to grow up the way he had, feeling unwanted or unloved.

He had to be the kind of father to his child that Archie's father had been to his own kids. The closest thing Kaspar had ever had to a father himself. He owed it to Archie. The woman whose door he suspected he would have been banging down months ago had he not kept the expanse of the Atlantic between them.

Which made no sense. Because that absolutely wasn't him. He didn't know what had come over him. The ghosts she had been resurrecting ever since that first night together when he'd realised who she was. When he hadn't been able to help himself from claiming her anyway.

It was all he could do to stay this side of the screen and not march around that blue curtain and demand to know exactly what was going on. But staying here was as much about trying not to crowd or frighten Archie as it was about stopping himself from trying to tell Catherine Jarvis how to do her job. As much as she might like and respect him, Catherine wouldn't think twice about calling him out for interfering where one of her patients was concerned.

'Right,' Catherine addressed Archie. 'Let's

clean you up and then you can sort yourself out. When you're ready, come back around and we can all have a bit of a chat.'

His stomach lurched. It was exactly the professional, calm tone he used when he suspected a serious issue but didn't want to worry anyone. Or perhaps it was his imagination.

It was strange, being this side of the proverbial table. He felt ill at ease, *lost*, and he didn't like it at all.

So how must Archie feel?

An unexpected wave of…*something* flooded through him. He'd told her that he wasn't about to play happy families. And that was true, he didn't want that. But there was something else there, too.

Had any other woman walked back into his life and declared herself pregnant with his child he might have expected to feel anger, resentment, and maybe there was a little of that with Archie. But there was something more. Like it was his duty to look after her. *To protect her?*

It was like a physical blow. For a moment all he could do was fight to maintain his balance, rocking on the balls of his feet. His whole career he'd fought for his patients. To the last moment and without exception. Because it was his duty, and because they mattered.

He'd felt a kind of protectiveness towards her as a kid, but that had been completely different. Certainly never in his entire adult life had he felt the urge to protect someone because he cared about *them*, on some...emotional level. He hadn't even thought he was capable of such an impulse.

What was he even to do with such sentimentality?

Unnerved, Kaspar thrust the plethora of questions from his head. He would concentrate on the medicine. That, at least, would make more sense. Sitting down, he forced himself to engage in polite conversation with his colleague, none of which he could recall even a minute later, and waited for Archie to appear.

The sight of her wan, nervous face twisted inside him. Instantly, he switched into cool surgeon mode.

'What did you find, Catherine?'

'Right. So, I did a full examination of you, Archana, and I would concur that you are approximately twenty weeks pregnant.'

'What is the issue?' Kaspar prompted sharply. This might not be his field of expertise but he wasn't considered a top surgeon for being oblivious to other fields. The way his colleague's examination had progressed, and the comments and questions she'd been asking didn't fit with a smooth, non-complicated pregnancy. Sure enough, she turned to him with an almost imperceptible nod. One colleague to another.

'I did see faint evidence of funnelling but I stress it *is* faint. I could send you for an MRI but I'd prefer to concentrate on the cervix length before making any firm decisions.' She turned back to Archie. 'However, I don't have a baseline length without calling your doctors and requesting your notes.'

Kaspar nodded, turning expectantly to Archie, whose expression was even more pinched and white. Instinctively, he reached out to take her icy-cold hand in his.

'Archie,' he prompted gently.

Slowly, so slowly, she turned her head to him, her eyes taking a little longer to focus.

'Archie, we need your doctors' details so that Catherine can contact them.'

'No one told me there was a problem.' Her voice was so quiet they had to strain to hear her.

'Archana.' Catherine's voice was gentle, coax-

ing. The way his usually was with other patients. But this wasn't *other patients*, this was
Archie. 'Would you like me to explain this in
more detail?'

Archie nodded stiffly. She didn't look at him
but her fingers gripped his surprisingly tightly.
Something shot through him, a powerful but
fleeting sensation. He couldn't identify it. He
wasn't even sure he wanted to.

'All right, during pregnancy the cervix, or the
neck of your womb, normally remains closed
and long, rather like a tube. As the pregnancy
progresses and you get ready to give birth, the
cervix begins to soften, shortening in length
and opening up.'

Catherine paused, waiting for confirmation
as Archie jerked her head in a semblance of a
nod.

He bit back his own questions. He couldn't
take over, he had to let Archie go at her own
pace.

'However,' Catherine continued gently as Archie mumbled a vague acknowledgement, 'in
your instance, there is evidence to suggest that
the neck of your womb might be shortening.
It's very faint and without knowing what the
measurements were at the start of your preg-

nancy I can't be sure. It isn't, at this point in time, less than twenty-five millimetres, which is the point at which I would usually advise having an emergency, or rescue, cervical suture. However, with your past history of miscarriage I would suggest that there is a high enough risk of premature delivery for me to consider performing the suture on you.'

'So...? We...wait?' Archie managed, frowning as if she was having trouble processing it all.

'For right now, yes. But we don't want to wait too much longer.' Catherine shook her head. 'After twenty-four weeks we don't usually perform cervical sutures either here in the US or back at your home in the UK. The standard of care for preemies is of such a high standard that it's generally considered that the risks of being born early is less than the risk to the baby of attempting to delay labour with an emergency suture.'

'So there are risks?'

For the first time, Archie's head snapped up, as though she was hauling herself back to reality by her very fingernails.

Kaspar felt a sliver of pride slip through him,

and he clasped her hand tighter as if that could somehow lend her strength.

'There are risks with any procedure,' his colleague answered, 'but particularly in an emergency procedure where the cervix has already shortened and is partly dilated. There's a risk of waters breaking and of infection developing. In your case, there's only faint evidence of effacement and no dilation.'

'But if I'm going to have it, it has to be now?' Archie asked tightly.

'As I said, I'd like a baseline measurement first, and we'll go from there.'

'Why didn't my doctor pick up on it?'

Her pained expression tugged and twisted at something inside him. He wasn't prepared for it. It was a strange, inner tussle not to jump in and grill Catherine on a much more detailed, medical level. Instead, he forced himself to continue sitting quietly, allowing Archie to go at her pace. The kind of questions he wanted to ask would only frighten her unnecessarily. They would deal with any other issues if and when they had to. Still, he would be calling Catherine as soon as he got a moment alone.

'As I said, it's very faint. This is my area of expertise...'

'They're supposed to be experts too...' Archie cut in, panicked, and, with an instinct he hadn't known he possessed, Kaspar found himself drawing her to him, making her meet his gaze. His voice quiet, level, as one might use to a frightened, cornered animal.

'Catherine is a highly specialised, world-class neonatal and maternal-foetal surgeon,' he soothed. 'We will deal with this. *She* will deal with it.'

'But if we miss it. If I don't have the...the...'

'Cervical suture,' he supplied evenly, wondering if this raging storm inside him was how every patient felt when they were sitting opposite him and *he* was the one delivering their diagnoses or prognoses.

'Right. If I don't have that then I lose this baby like I did before?'

'There's no way to know,' continued Catherine. 'You're past the point at which the previous miscarriage occurred. However, there is some evidence that your cervix *might* be beginning to efface. It's possible you could go to term like this, without any intervention. I can't be sure. I need more information. In cases like yours, where it isn't clear, the suture is usually only put in if there's a history of two or more late miscarriages or premature births.'

'Lose two babies?' Archie gasped, horrified. 'Before they will do anything? No. No, I can't lose another baby. I can't.'

'I know it's hard, I'm sorry. But sometimes we have to be sure,' Catherine was saying, but he couldn't sit quietly any longer.

'If Archie doesn't have the cervical suture and then after that twenty-four-week mark begins to go into labour, you'll do what?' he asked his colleague sharply. 'Pessaries?'

'Yes.' She nodded, turning her focus back to Archie. 'If that is the case, then we would probably offer you progesterone or pessaries instead. As you mentioned during the examination, they tried an Arabin pessary with your first baby.'

'Which didn't work,' Archie choked out as Catherine bobbed her head, again softly.

'And that's why I'd like to request your medical records from your doctor to determine whether a cervical suture might be a sensible precaution.'

'And it will stop me from losing my baby?'

'There's no guarantee. Research into how well cervical sutures stop preterm birth is always ongoing, but it is thought to reduce the risk of early delivery by significant percentages. Once I have more information, I'll bring you back for a further examination and we'll discuss things in greater depth if we feel we might go ahead.'

'But...'

The pleading in her tone twisted at Kapar's gut, but he couldn't indulge it. He had to be the strong one.

'Archie, give Catherine your doctors' contact details. Once she has your full notes she can make a more informed decision and, I promise you, we'll answer every single one of your questions then.'

'Right.' Catherine shot him a grateful look. 'You have full insurance?'

'No...' She froze, as if she hadn't really thought that far ahead.

'The medical expenses will be covered,' Kaspar cut in firmly.

He'd pay for it out of his own pocket if necessary.

'And she's staying with you?'

'Yes.'

He ignored Archie as she glowered at him.

'Good.' Catherine nodded, holding out a form for Archie's medical contact details.

Grimly he took it, coaxing the information out of Archie, line by line. And when it was finally done, he helped her up, sorted out her scant belongings, and led her out of his colleague's office with a word of thanks.

She looked dazed, thrown. The exact way he felt. But he refused to give in to it. He couldn't afford to. If it sucked him in, he'd be no use to Archie, and right now he knew she needed him more than ever.

'I didn't come here for your money,' Archie muttered as she found herself being ushered out of the office. Her mind was grappling for some diversion, however banal, from the bone-gripping terror that she might lose this baby the way she'd lost Faith.

'Or for you to house me,' she added absently.

She had given Dr Jarvis the right name, hadn't she? The right address for her doctor's surgery?

'What should I have said, Archie? That you jumped on a plane and came out here wholly unprepared?'

She pursed her lips, his tone exactly what

she'd feared when she'd been halfway across the Atlantic. The accusation out before she could stop it.

'You'd rather I hadn't told you about the baby.'

'That isn't what I said.' He blew out an angry breath and, for one moment, if she hadn't known it to be impossible she would have thought he was as confused as she was.

'I'll stay in a hotel.' It was hard to summon some semblance of pride when all she wanted to do was break down on his shoulder and howl.

Kaspar let out a scornful snort.

'You're pregnant. With my baby. You will remain with me. For the duration. It isn't up for debate, Archana.'

'There is no *duration*. What you and Catherine seem to be forgetting is that I don't come from here, and besides I can't afford medical care. I need to go back home and I need to speak to my own doctors.'

'You can't just run away,' Kaspar snapped. 'And as for medical costs, I will deal with that. You won't be going back to the UK while you're pregnant. In fact, you won't be going back at all.'

'Sorry? What?' she asked. Very calmly. Very deliberately.

She couldn't possibly have heard that correctly.

Did it make it better, or worse, that he looked equally stupefied?

'You won't be returning to the UK,' he said slowly, as if he wasn't really sure of the words coming out of his own mouth.

It was disconcerting to see the famously focussed Kaspar Athari uncertain about anything.

'I... I...' Archie was aware that, for a moment, she opened and closed her mouth feeling much like the fish in the calming tank in the luxurious waiting area outside. Finally, her voice came back. 'I can assure you that is *exactly* what I'll be doing. It's where my flat is, my career, my *life*.'

'Except that now you're carrying my baby.'

'I had noticed.' Her heart pounded so loudly she was afraid it was ready to slam its way right out of her chest. 'But you told me we wouldn't be playing happy families.'

'That was before.'

The conversation was all too similar to the one she'd had when her ex-husband had told her about his job opportunity in Zurich. She'd known then that there was no way she wanted to leave the UK, that her life *was* there. This time she heard the words but she didn't feel the same passion.

She told herself the difference was the baby. Not Kaspar.

It couldn't be him. She couldn't afford to let it be. She turned on him.

'Before what?'

'Just...before,' he ground out. 'I don't know, Archie. You need to give me time. You've had months to get your head around this pregnancy. I've barely had a couple of hours. You'll stay here until I have a plan.'

She could see what it cost him to admit to her that he, Kaspar Athari, had no idea what to do right at this moment. She could more than relate. But she couldn't afford to crumble right now, much as she might want to. Much as the weaker Archie wanted to lean on him, even cling to him. She forced her head up.

'I can't stay here forever. I think Immigration might have something to say about that.'

Far from throwing Kaspar, her words seemed to galvanise him. The powerful, authoritative man the world knew was coming back. Shutting out once and for all that tiny glimpse she'd seen of a remotely vulnerable side to him.

'We'll sort that out.' His disdainful rebuttal was aggravating. 'We'll have to. You're carrying my baby. My blood. Which means, whether I like it or not, you're now my family. And I'll do whatever I need to in order to keep my family with me. I won't allow this baby to grow up thinking she wasn't wanted. Feeling she doesn't have a home.'

'It...*he* will have a home,' she bit out, remembering at the last moment their agreement not to call the baby *it*. Surely there was no doubt that Kaspar's current autocratic attitude stemmed as much from whatever horrors lay in his childhood as that *it* label had been?

'His home is with me. The mother.'

'And with me. The father,' he said, narrowing his eyes at her. 'I will not be an absent father. You can't push me out of this, Archie.'

'I'm not.' Her voice was too loud, too fractured, but at least she now knew she was right about Kaspar's past dictating his actions now. 'You're the father. I wanted you to know. I felt I owed it to you, to the baby, to give you the choice of being part of its life. But... I can't give up my whole life just to stay in the States with you. I can't even work out here, for one thing.'

'I can take care of you.'

'Out of what? A sense of duty?' she challenged. 'Not because you *want* me. Or our baby.'

'What difference does it make?' And it was only at that instant that she realised just how desperately she wished he could tell her otherwise. 'I *will* take care of you. Both of you.'

'I don't want to be taken care of.'

'Make your mind up, Archie.' His barbed tone pierced its way through her, lodging inside her, twisting painfully. 'An hour or so ago when I said you'd always been a strong kid, you were telling me how fragile you were. Now you're telling me you can handle everything yourself?'

'That isn't what I said.' Archie threw her hands up. He was distorting things, confusing her. Or was he right? Was *she* confusing things? She tried again. 'I want to be...cared for. Not cosseted.'

'And I will be a part of my child's life.'

'I'm not saying you can't be...'

It was infuriating. And yet, somehow, it was

also reassuring. The fact that he was planning for the baby's—*their* baby's—future. As though it had one. As though the fact that she might lose it the way she'd lost Faith wasn't even a possibility for him. It was what she'd needed. He made her feel strong again. Just like he had a hundred—a thousand—times before. As a kid. Even if he didn't remember it.

Suddenly she was tired of fighting. And scared. And it was making it harder and harder for her to think straight. Words began floating around her head. The risks she hadn't even known about a few hours ago were now threatening to overwhelm her.

She really could lose this baby the way she'd lost *Faith*. Having her suspicions had been one thing, but to hear it so unequivocally was another.

She longed for him to fold his strong arms around her and pull her to his huge chest, comforting her and caring for her, as though he really wanted to. Not just out of some sense of moral decency. But he didn't. They simply stood there, pretending they weren't squaring off against each other.

'I want you to be a part of our baby's life, Kaspar,' she said softly. 'A big part. But I can't stay here. Your life is here and that's fine. But mine isn't. And for what it's worth, I don't see you offering to give up *your* life and *your* work to follow me permanently to the UK, where you could also be with your child on a daily basis.'

Kaspar sighed. 'We both know that your work is more relocatable than mine is. I have teams here that depend on me, patients that trust me to be there throughout their care.'

Archie scowled, though she knew he had a point. As much as she loved her job, it was fairly flexible, and unlike his it wasn't a matter of life or death. 'You just think your life is more important than mine,' she finished petulantly, in spite of herself.

His dismissive shrug didn't help.

'There is no *your* life and *my* life. Not now. You're carrying my baby so whatever our individual lives were like in the past, that's all gone now. Like it or not, it's *our* lives. I will not be apart from my child.' Misery was etched into every line, every contour on his unfairly handsome face. 'I won't have her growing up the way I did, pulled between one parent and the other.'

His unexpectedly searing admission ate at her.

Archie began to speak, then hesitated. She had to choose her words very, very carefully. She reached out to touch his chest, steeling herself for the jolt of awareness that charged through her even before she made contact. Even prepared for it, even now, she couldn't make herself immune to him.

That was another thing she was going to work on.

'We're not your parents. If we both want to be with this baby, we'll find a solution. It... *he*...will know he's wanted. We don't have to be in the same country but we do have to work it out carefully and fairly.'

'I want to be in my child's life. Every day.' He covered her hand with his, but didn't even seem to notice what he was doing. Still, it stole her breath away.

'It doesn't have to be that way,' she began, but he cut her off.

'You'll move in with me, Archie. For all intents and purposes, this child will have a proper family.'

Without warning, her heart flip-flopped in her chest. It was worrying how much the notion appealed to her. How close she was to agreeing to such a ridiculous idea. But as much as she tried to back up both physically and mentally, she could no more remove her hand from the compelling heat of his body than she could refuse outright.

'But we won't be a proper family, will we?' It was meant to be a demand, but her voice was far breathier than she would have liked. Sadness and regret still lined his face.

'Of course not,' he scoffed, oblivious to the fact that he found it so easy to slam all her pitiable dreams away with those three words. 'But our child will at least have a mother and father around who don't want to kill each other on a daily basis. And that's more than I ever had.'

'I don't want to settle for that.' She barely recognised her own shaky voice. 'I want so much more. I want love. I want to be cherished. I want what my father always told me he and my mother had before she died, but which I was too young to remember.'

He shut her down, clearly not listening to her.

'This subject isn't up for discussion, Archana. You're coming home with me and we'll work out the rest from there.'

And before she could respond any further Kaspar was gone and she was alone. In the middle of an empty corridor.

CHAPTER SEVEN

KASPAR'S HOME WAS everything she should have expected and so much...well, *less*.

It was stunning. Modern glass, sleek design and cool granite perched atop a slight hillside overlooking a private, tantalising beach. As if he was showing her all he could offer their child that she never could.

Archie stared up into the double-height ceiling space of the main living area. All gleaming white and black metal, framing enormous windows that offered breathtaking views across the sea and off into the horizon.

Gorgeous.

It was also completely and utterly soulless. As if no one lived here at all. The perfect show home. Which only proved to her that it wasn't all about money. She cradled her belly protectively. It was about love, and stability, both of which she could provide.

Strong foundations. Dependable.

Could Kaspar?

She doubted it. Or perhaps that was just her own bias since everything he did left her wound too tightly to even think straight. It hadn't escaped her that ever since he had walked out into that corridor when she'd been trying to pluck up the courage to knock on the door, her body had filled with a low, faint humming. Desire. Need.

One afternoon with the man was all it had taken to convince her that she wasn't over anything. That a part of her still hankered for him. Even now. That realisation alone should have told her that she needed to stay as far away from Kaspar as possible. Certainly not spend even one night at his home.

But he'd terrified her by taking her to see Dr Jarvis. Reinforcing every last fear she'd spent five months telling herself was simply in her head. That what had happened with Faith wouldn't happen again.

For all her earlier arguing, the car journey home had given her time to calm down. Time to acknowledge that she would stay with Kaspar as long as she needed to if it meant her baby would be all right. In many ways she was more grateful to Kaspar than she could ever have anticipated. He didn't have to help her, there'd been nothing compelling him to get her in to see his colleague. He'd always made it clear to the media that he didn't have any intention of settling down or having a family. He could have thanked her for telling him and let her return to the UK.

But that wasn't Kaspar.

It was reassuring to know she hadn't misjudged him five months ago.

'There's a guest suite through those doors over there.' Kaspar cut across her thoughts as he headed back down across the hallway to a different set of doors. 'I'll be through that way.'

She gripped the large, rather masculine-looking, leather wingback chair in front of her.

'You're going?'

'I have to get showered and changed.' He frowned. 'I've got a charity dinner event tonight. I'm a guest speaker.'

'Okay.'

'Do you need me to stay?'

A part of her wanted to say yes. A bigger part of her knew the time to herself would be welcome. She forced a bright smile.

'No. I could do with the evening to myself. Besides, you can't let people down.'

He nodded, unsmiling.

'I would prefer not to. But if I wasn't speaking, I wouldn't go.'

'Should I...? Do I...come with you?'

He looked entirely unimpressed. She tried not to let it get to her.

'I hardly think that's the best idea. Aside from the fact that you're meant to be resting, tonight is a high-profile event and being photographed out with me—especially looking like...*that*...' he gestured to her baby bump '...is the quickest way to get people nosing into every single facet of our lives. I can't imagine you want to see yourself splashed across the entertainment news headlines tomorrow morning, do you?'

'No, of course not.' Archie blinked, attempting to command her faithless heart not to read so much into the way he'd said *our lives.*

As if it implied some form of...togetherness.

'Good.' He nodded, satisfied, although she thought he might have had the decency not to look quite so smug. 'Then you'll stay here, keeping a low profile.'

He was gone before she could answer, leaving Archie alone to explore her new surroundings at her apparent leisure. Instead, she could only stare at the closed door and wonder where they were supposed to go from here.

She needed a distraction. Something to take her fears off the idea of losing this baby, something to ground her and remind her of the strong woman she was in other arenas of her life.

Like in the workplace. Yes, that was it. She could work, she'd brought her laptop. She was lucky that the nature of her job meant she could work from any number of sites or offices— emails and video conferencing were practically *de rigueur*. Certainly at this stage of the project. And she was lucky that she'd worked with the commercial manager on so many projects before over the years that he knew how reliable and fastidious she'd always been. Still, hopping on a plane to different country wasn't exactly usual practice. If she was going to keep her job then she would need to do some work for as long as she was out here.

And she would need a job to get back to once the baby was born. How else was she supposed to keep a roof over their heads? Because no matter what Kaspar had said back in the hospital, it wasn't practical for them to live together and pretend to be some kind of family, even for the sake of their baby.

She booted up her laptop, the waiting emails a welcome diversion as she fired off a handful of easy responses before working on a couple of more carefully worded letters to contractors and the client. But after a few hours the words began to swim before her eyes, the grid patterns of the spreadsheets all merging into each other. And, instead, Kaspar's face began to creep back into her head.

It couldn't be a good thing that all she could think about was him. And their baby. He was insisting on taking control, the way he always had seemed to do, but what kind of a *real* father would he allow himself to be?

The realisation clung to her mind.

She'd never appreciated, growing up, just how badly his parents' volatile relationship had damaged Kaspar. What if he couldn't get past that? What if he carried it into any relationship with their own baby? With her?

It was as though in asking herself that first question, she'd opened the floodgates for a hundred more to rush into her brain.

She'd never realised just how deeply his parents had influenced him before. She'd known a bit, growing up, but her father had shielded her from a lot. Had she been completely naïve in clinging to her memory of the sweet, sensitive young boy she had once known, who had looked to her own father as more of a role model than anyone else?

She couldn't bear the idea that, in time, Kaspar might come to resent her if she and the baby impacted too heavily on his life.

What if he dated other women?

Something spiked inside her, like the stinging slice of a razor-sharp blade, even as she told herself that it didn't matter to her either way. She told herself that what he did in his personal life was no more her business now than it ever had been. It wouldn't make any difference to her. She would have him to thank for the most precious gift he could ever have given her.

Archie slammed the laptop lid down without even thinking about what she was doing. She could tell herself she didn't care all she liked. She didn't buy a word of it. Not even for a second.

What Kaspar did mattered to her. It shouldn't, but it did. And the longer she stayed in his company the more hurt she was going to wind up getting. It was inevitable. Inexorable.

And yet there was no way she could leave. Not to go to a hotel, and certainly not to return to the UK. Not after what she'd discovered today. The very life of her unborn baby now depended on Kaspar, and how he could help her, and she'd walk over coals searing enough to melt the soles of her feet if it meant not going through the agony of another hateful miscarriage.

She'd just have to find a way to seal her heart, her mind off from Kaspar. Think of him as a business deal. The father of her baby but, ultimately, nothing to do with her.

That couldn't be too hard. Could it?

Kaspar dodged yet another nameless woman—he'd lost count of how many had tried to corner him this evening—and glowered at the auctioneer who was delighting the crowd as he chaired the charity auction.

It was a successful evening, even pleasant, but he couldn't enjoy a moment of it. His thoughts were centred around Archie, their baby and the unwelcome news Catherine had delivered.

He wondered what Archie was doing now. Still working on her laptop, as she'd been when he'd left her? So focussed and wrapped up in her work that she hadn't even noticed him leaving. It was ironic, the one thing he strived for in himself, admired in others, was the thing he was already beginning to resent in Archie.

Because he didn't need her to tell him what that driven expression on her face meant. He recognised it. It told him she was determined to maintain her job, and therefore her life, back in the UK. That she intended to return with his baby as soon as she could, despite everything he'd said to her about not wanting to be an absent father.

He hadn't even realised how strongly he'd felt when he'd first uttered those words. But the fact of it was that it was true. The idea of losing them was unimaginable. *No.* Kaspar pulled himself up short. It was *unacceptable.*

The temptation to go home and tell Archie exactly that was almost overwhelming. There was only one thing stopping him. He needed something more compelling than words. He needed to prove to her that he would do anything for this baby. He needed to prove to her that he *wanted* this baby.

No easy feat when, if anyone had asked him twelve hours ago how he felt about having a baby, he would have laughed in their face. He'd never wanted children, or a family, or a wife. He'd been content to play the genius surgeon, perennial bad boy, who would never inflict himself on anyone the way his parents had inflicted their distasteful, damaging vitriol on either their son or themselves.

For decades he'd told himself that the best thing he could ever do for any child was to ensure that he wasn't their father. No child should ever have to endure the upbringing of his own youth. Pushed from one volatile parent to the other, a pawn in their explosive games. Unwanted and in the way, even when his mother had suddenly realised that it might help his father's career, and hurt hers, if she didn't drag her unhappy fifteen-year-old with her.

And then Archie had knocked on his door and his whole world had shifted on its axis.

He was going to be a father.

Possibly.

Without warning a terrible tightness coiled through him, as unfamiliar as it was uncomfortable. For a moment he couldn't identify it at all, and then it dawned on him. It was fear. And powerlessness.

Everything that Catherine had said this afternoon had made sense to him *medically*. But now that the initial shock was wearing off, his brain was finally locking onto the fact that this wasn't any baby they were discussing, this was *his* baby. His and Archie's.

He wanted this baby to be safe and he wanted to provide the loving family he had never had.

The fact that Archie had made it abundantly clear that she would rather cross the Atlantic, swimming the entire way if she had to, than have him be a daily part of her baby's life cut him deeper than he would prefer to acknowledge. It scraped at him like nothing else ever had.

He'd thought he'd long since got over the pain of not being wanted. By his mother, his father and, to some extent, his best friend Robbie when they'd fallen out over some girl whose name he couldn't even remember any more. *Sarah* perhaps? *Suki? Sadie?* Not that it even mattered.

But Archie's rejection of him ate into him far, far deeper. She'd done her duty by telling him she was pregnant, but she evidently now wanted to be as far away from him as she possibly could get. And he didn't want to let her go. Not just, he suspected, as an image of her breathtaking smile and dancing eyes filled his head while his insides hitched, for the health of their baby. The restlessness he felt whenever he was around her was like an ache of desire.

It made no sense. He was losing his mind and Archie was the one making him lose it. She threatened the order he had created around himself, blurred his clearly set-out parameters, and blasted away his peace of mind.

He could pretend he had been strong all afternoon for Archie's sake, but he was terribly suspicious that the truth was that he needed to stay strong for himself just as much. What he really needed was a plan. Something that would keep his unexpected family around him, allow him to be the father his baby deserved.

Something with which Archie couldn't possibly argue.

'Do you promise to love, honour, cherish and protect...?'

Archie stared at the registrar as though her soul was wholly disconnected from her body. As though she was one of the witnesses, who she didn't even know but apparently Kaspar did, watching the brief ceremony, rather than the not-so-blushing bride standing opposite a grim-faced Kaspar and clutching a small bouquet that was so jaunty and bright it seemed to mock her.

She felt numb. As numb as she'd felt when Kaspar had returned home from the fundraiser early the other night and issued his edict.

Even now she could recall exactly how her body had felt, as though it had been too small to contain her, squeezing her until every last breath had been crushed out of her. And yet Kaspar had looked, for all the world, as though he was relaying something as banal as the weather.

'Marriage?' she had whispered, a lump of something that was halfway between desolation and fury, or perhaps a combination of the two, lodged in her throat. 'We'll never get a license.'

'This is California, there's no waiting time. A long line could mean a two hour wait, but that's about it.' He brushed her concern aside with a sweep of his arm. 'Then we have ninety days to actually get married before the license expires, so unless you're planning on some elaborate ceremony somewhere, I know a couple of ministers who can perform marriages. Either one of them would be happy to step in at such short notice for us. I'm sure we can even go to the beach if you'd prefer something more... romantic.'

He pulled a face which wasn't exactly encouraging. She tried again.

'I'm not Californian. I'm not even American.'

'You don't have to be a resident.' Again, he dismissed her with apparent ease. 'And there's no restriction against foreigners marrying here either. You just need the correct documentation which you have. I've already checked. '

'Kaspar...'

'There's no other way.' His crisp response had been damning. 'But if you need another reason, then how about this; you need to be here where you can be seen by Catherine and my health insurance will cover you only if you are my wife.'

She had savings. Money she'd set aside year in and year out as her rainy-day fund. But nothing that might cover something like this. She'd hated to put it to Kaspar, but she'd had little choice.

'What if you paid?' She could actually remember running her tongue over her teeth in an effort to free them from her top lip. 'I would pay you back. Every penny...or at least every cent...in time, of course.'

'No.'

'Please, Kaspar?' It wasn't like he wasn't wealthy enough to afford it. Although she hadn't been able to say that, it would have sounded so cold-blooded, and that wasn't how she would have intended it. Her voice had dropped to a whisper. 'Why not?'

'Why should I pay out of my pocket just so you can run back to England and take my child away from me at the first chance you get?' he had ground out, and if she hadn't known better she might have thought he sounded almost urgent. But then his commanding tone had come back and she'd known she'd just imagined it. 'I told you, this baby will be brought up knowing her father.'

Archie blinked as she realised that, back in the present, the minister was looking at her expectantly. She clutched the flowers tighter and prayed her subconscious was paying enough attention to know what stage of the ceremony they were up to.

'I do,' she choked out, relieved when he bobbed his head, turning back to Kaspar. 'Repeat after me. I, Kaspar Athari…'

She tried to concentrate, but it was too much. Her head still swam with memories of that night. She had assured him that their baby would know him. Promised him. But he had been intransigent, his cool, level responses only heightening her agitation.

She hadn't known why the idea of marriage had disconcerted her so much. She'd told herself it was because the idea was ludicrous, but feared it was more because a part of her actually longed to say yes. To take the easy solution that he was offering. To accept the safe stability of a marriage. A unit.

But how long would that safe stability last? Especially with a man like Kaspar, who had spent his life vigorously avoiding ties of any kind.

As if he could read her thoughts, he had thrust his hands into his pockets, looking, for all the world, like the conversation bored him.

'I don't work on promises, Archie. I never promise my patients or their families anything that I can't one hundred percent guarantee. I prefer to put in place assurances.'

'And marrying me is an assurance?'

'The closest I can get, yes.' He'd given a light shrug. 'You can't deny me, or the baby, that way.'

She'd told herself that it couldn't be happening. That it wasn't fair. She'd resisted the urge to run from the room, knowing that it might offer her relief for a moment or two but that ultimately she couldn't escape Kaspar. Or the conversation.

'Please. I'll give you any other assurances you want. Sign any contract you put in front of me.'

'Of course you will. It will be called a marriage contract.'

'No.' Her vehemence had turned Kaspar's eyes to hard, opal gleams. As though she'd hurt him. But such a notion was ludicrous.

'If the idea of marrying me is that abhorrent to you, Archana, then surely you can see how I might think you'd leave with our baby the first chance you get.'

But wasn't that exactly what the problem was? That she *didn't* find the idea of marriage to Kaspar so abhorrent. Or at least she only abhorred the idea of a loveless marriage to him. She could tell herself it was because she'd been there and done that. She'd made the mistake of thinking the way she and Joe had cared for each other had been enough. But it hadn't, and she didn't want to go through that again. Certainly not with Kaspar.

Because the truth, as much as she'd tried to deny it until now, was that a part of her—a small, childish remnant from her youth, no doubt—was in love with him. And being married to him, without him loving her back in any way, would be too much to bear. How could she stand the fact that he would never be *hers*? Even if she married him?

Kaspar Athari was his own man. He would never belong to any one. And she wanted so much more than that from him.

Archie paused as the celebrant turned to her now. Her turn to repeat the vows. She didn't even recognise her own voice. The ceremony could have been happening to someone else. She was still stuck there, in her own head, stuck back in that night.

In her urgency, she'd even asked him exactly what marriage to him would look like. She didn't know what she'd hoped he would say. It certainly hadn't been the casual shoulder hunch he'd offered. The nonchalant, *'Why don't we cross that bridge when we come to it?'*

There certainly hadn't been any words of love, or even affection. There and then she'd promised herself that she would never settle for half-measures, with Kaspar or with anyone else. If she couldn't have all of him, she wanted none. She'd done half-measures before and look where that had got her. She refused to do it again.

In her mind's eye, Archie could see herself heading resolutely across the room. But it was no good. By the time she'd reached the door she'd stopped, her hand on the handle but still not turning around.

'I can't marry you, Kaspar. I've made that mistake before. And I can't make you help me,' she'd whispered again, desperately summoning the strength to turn the door handle. 'But I'm begging you to do so.'

He had crossed the room, the heat of his body like a wall behind her, searing her as his hand had covered hers and drawn it from the cold metal.

'Are you so sure it would be a mistake?' The rawness in his voice had been like a rasp against her heart.

Archie had wanted to tell him that of course it would be a mistake. She'd known she shouldn't cave. But his question had sounded so skinned, like an exposed wound, his hand had still been holding hers and she could still *feel* his body so close to her. She remembered dropping her head, then in defiance of all logic she'd turned and faced him.

The pinched expression on his face had taken her aback. As though she'd wounded him. As though he actually cared. She'd wondered if she could be wrong about him. If he could really want her in his life. As his wife.

She'd averted her eyes but his other hand had slid instantly beneath her chin, his fingers had tilted her head up and forced her to look at him.

'My baby will want for nothing,' he'd stated firmly, fiercely. 'I'll make sure of that. Neither will you, but your lives are here now. With me. I'm not your idiot ex-husband who let you walk away from him. I suggest you don't make the blunder of mistaking me for him.'

She hadn't been about to tell him that was hardly likely. That no one could mistake Kaspar for anyone but himself. His utter certainty had been mesmerising. No wonder people rarely refused him. Including her. *Especially* her.

'Love should be the core of your marriage.' The registrar smiled benevolently now. 'Love is the reason you are here. But it also will take trust to know in your hearts that you want the best for each other.'

She tuned out again. Joe might never have been enough to compel her to leave her life for Zurich. But Kaspar was so much she wondered if she might even leave her life to follow him to the very bowels of hell.

The notion had terrified her. Kaspar didn't love her or want her, he only wanted their baby. Abruptly she'd heard herself lashing out. Wanting to wind Kaspar the way he had done to her.

'I should never have come here,' she'd blurted out, hugging her laptop in front of her chest like it had been some form of body armour against Kaspar's words. 'I should never have told you about the baby. You ruin everything.'

She hadn't been even remotely prepared for the look of absolute pain and devastation that had tugged at his features. She'd opened her mouth to apologise, to find some way to take it back, but then it was as though he'd sucked all the misery back in and instead a wave of fury had smashed over her, emanating from him like a thick, black, lethal cloud.

'You won't take my baby away, Archie.' His ferocity had been unmistakeable. 'You won't shut me out of my child's life, or leave her thinking for a single moment that I didn't want to be there for her. This is my baby, too. I will be a part of every aspect of things. Not some weekend or holiday father but a proper dad, who is there for the first word, the first step, the first dry night.'

She'd tried to take it back. Guilt and regret had almost overwhelmed her. She'd opened her mouth to tell him she had never meant those words that had tumbled, so cruelly, out of her mouth. But the apology hadn't come, and anyway Kaspar wouldn't have let her.

'This isn't about you or me, it's about the life of this baby,' he'd hissed out, his voice lethal. 'You need medical supervision, which is here, with me. This is non-negotiable.'

And that had been the end of it. Those words, uttered in what felt like a lifetime ago.

Now, a few days later, they were here, and Archie was gazing at a grim Kaspar. She gaped as the registrar beamed his widest smile yet.

'I now declare you to be husband and wife.'

The worst thing was that a part of her was only too eager to comply.

CHAPTER EIGHT

'DID YOU CALL that a kiss?' Kaspar demanded as they stepped back into his…*their* home a scant few hours later.

He didn't know why he was trying to tease her. Perhaps because now they were married he knew they finally needed to get past the animosity that had settled on them. Black, heavy and cold. They had to move on from it.

It was one of the reasons he'd arranged for them to have their wedding breakfast at a private, fine dining experience in one of LA's most exclusive restaurants. It was his attempt at an olive branch, but he hadn't accounted for how entrenched they had become.

The silence at their table, the scrape of metal against fine china, the hollow clink of crystal wine glasses, both filled with water, had only emphasised the emptiness of the day, until finally Kaspar was able to bear it no more.

'I know you're not sure about this marriage,'

he sighed, covering her hand lightly with his across the table, 'and I'm sorry if you feel I pushed you into it. Seeing you in front of the minister looking so sad...well, that isn't what I want. Please,' he implored her, and in his eyes she saw an unexpected flash of the vulnerable, proud boy she had once known. 'Let's try to make this thing work, let's try to make our home a pleasant one, if nothing else. The baby deserves that much.'

Archie's heart sank a little. Of course it was the baby he was really worried about, but she nodded anyway, and in a small, tight voice agreed. 'I can be pleasant.'

'Thank you.'

Now, though, as they walked down the hallway of the beach house, Kaspar tried for a little more levity. 'I know you can kiss far better than you showed me today.'

Archie tilted her chin up at him, utterly elegant and poised. It gave him an unmistakeable kick to realise that he could see straight through her. He could read her in a way he'd never expected to be able to.

'It may shock you to know this, Kaspar, but

I don't want to kiss you again. I certainly don't want to sleep with you.'

He grinned unexpectedly. The first in days.

'I was talking about a kiss. Who said anything about sleeping together?'

'I surmised it was where you were going with the conversation.' She flushed, struggling hard not to sound so prim. Too hard.

'I hadn't been. Interesting it was where *your* mind went, though.'

'My mind went nowhere untoward, I can assure you.'

Something like relief skittered across her face and Kaspar realised it was a game. One designed to speak to his basest instincts. She was wriggling under his skin, the way she'd always been able to as a kid. Only there was nothing childlike about the attraction that now fizzed between them.

'Is that so?'

'That's so,' she confirmed, but her voice quivered.

'Are you sure?'

She didn't answer and his gaze held hers, missing nothing. Not her quick, shallow breathing, or the flush creeping up her neck, or the way she tried to swallow so discreetly. For a moment there was nothing. No sound, no movement. Then, suddenly, without even thinking, he closed the gap between them and hauled her body to his and wrapped his hand around her hair to tip her head backwards until she was staring up at him.

She didn't speak. He suspected she couldn't, and that send a shot of pure triumph jolting through him. And then he was crushing her mouth to his and a thousand glorious, dazzling fireworks were going off in his head all at once. Greedy and demanding, he feasted on her and she responded willingly. Wantonly. Her body, bump and all, pressed to him, her tongue dancing to his tune, her hands reaching for his powerful shoulders. And when she moaned against his lips his whole body tightened in response, everything shining that much brighter in his mind.

If he didn't stop this now, he feared he would never be able to do so. She was too damned intoxicating. Still, he didn't know how he succeeded to drop his arm or move away from her. He had no idea how he managed to hold his ground as she stood there, swaying and confused. It was a battle to talk as though he wasn't every bit as affected by the kiss as she clearly was.

'You're right, your disinclination to have sex with me again is abundantly clear,' he taunted softly, feeling bizarrely exhilarated as the oddest sense of calm seemed to permeate his body.

It didn't matter that Archie was staring at him as though he had lost his mind, and it didn't matter that even though he could see the jumble of thoughts that were barging through her head, he felt oddly detached. Confident. *Right*. A whisper of euphoria curled inexplicably through him.

'You had no right to do that,' she choked out eventually. 'I don't want you to do that.'

'Then you shouldn't kiss me back so willingly,' he responded, offering no room for argument.

Not another. Not when he was already feeling so rattled. And yet so triumphant. He felt another chunk of ice fall away.

'Marriage isn't what you wanted when you came here,' he told her quietly. 'I know that. Just as I know you gave me a thousand reasons why it was insane. But we're married now and those reasons don't matter. *You* don't matter. I don't matter. All that matters is our baby. And that he or she has the childhood, the life that you had. Not the one that I had.'

'How would I know that much about your childhood?' she bit back. 'I saw a little but my father kept his confidences. Mostly, I know the rumours from the press. Now I'm your wife. But how can I begin to really understand?'

He had no intention of answering, certainly not in a way that invited investigation of his life, but suddenly he heard himself speaking.

'What do you want to know?'

'You would tell me?' Wide, round eyes pinned him down. It was all he could to get a response out.

'Ask.'

She visibly deflated. Her anger seeped out of her and into the ether so suddenly it was though it had never existed. Still, he wasn't prepared for her fingers to suddenly reach out and skim his cheek.

'What happened, Kaspar?' she murmured. 'I know your mother was volatile, selfish. I know both your parents were. But what is it that I *don't* know?'

She was asking him to trust her enough to open up with the one thing he'd never told anyone. Not ever. His entire life.

He drew in one deep, steadying breath. Then another. And all the while she stood there, her eyes locked with his and her fingers resting on his cheek, so lightly that he wasn't sure if he could feel them or merely sense them.

Everything in him railed at the mere thought of revisiting those hateful memories, let alone voicing them aloud, reliving them. But he'd offered. He couldn't renege now.

Wordlessly, he led her into the living room. It took an eternity for them both to settle. And then she sat, staring at him. Half expectant, half just waiting for him to shut her out instead.

He wasn't sure where to even start. As if she could read his mind, Archie tried to prompt him.

'Robbie met your parents once. Or at least saw them dropping you off once at boarding school. He...said they wasn't exactly...loving.'

He swallowed a bark of bitter laughter. Let it burn the back of his throat. Used it to propel him forward the way he always had done.

'They wouldn't have been remotely loving.' His voice was more clipped than he might have liked, but that couldn't be helped. 'Love didn't exist in our home. At least not towards me.

Which I think was a step up from my parents' twisted version of *love*.'

'But you were their son.' She looked dazed.

'I wasn't wanted. Not like you and Robbie. I was a mistake.'

'That's how you felt?'

'That's what they called me.' He let out a humourless laugh. 'It was one of their more restrained names for me. The only time they really referred to me was to call me names or to fight about whose turn it was to take responsibility for me. I was rarely a *he*, I was most often an *it*.'

Cold realisation flowed through her.

'Which is why you got so mad when I called our baby *it*.'

'I couldn't stand it,' he admitted. 'The memories were so strong when you did that, that a sense of worthlessness that ran through me, even all these years later.'

'Were they…as volatile as the press makes out?' she pressed cautiously.

How could she already have grown to hate that expression that clouded his face? To detest his parents for putting it there? It occurred to her that she'd seen it once before. The first summer Robbie had invited him to stay at their house. Too late, she remembered the introverted, awkward seven-year-old he'd been back then.

'You don't have to answer that,' she blurted out suddenly.

Her entire body felt like it was combusting as he cupped her chin gently as if to reassure her.

'You know when Hollywood make films and they're horrific and poignant and the world says how it makes them think, and yet the truth is that it doesn't even come close to how appalling the real truth actually was? Well, that's what the media have reported my life and parents' marriage to be versus the reality.'

'They've always called it explosive.' She frowned.

'And then they've dressed it up to be something sensationalist and implied that such uncontrolled passion was somehow romantic and dramatic,' he ground out. 'But the truth was that there was nothing romantic or sensational about it. It was ugly and twisted and destructive. What's your first memory, Archie?'

It was a fight to keep his voice even, not to let the bitterness creep in. Nonetheless, Archie bit her lip as she slowly bobbed her head.

'It's probably not a real memory, just a memory I've cobbled together from photos and the stories my father told me. But it's of my mother helping me to paint a wooden race cart my father had made for me. It was just before she died so I was probably about six. Then we went out onto the dirt track behind our house and Robbie and I raced each other while my mother refereed and my father pushed me to help me keep up with Robbie.'

His chest cracked even as he knew that such special memories were exactly what he wanted for his child. For the baby Archie was now carrying.

'Mine is of my parents screaming at each other as my mother accused my father of not wanting her to succeed in Hollywood because he wouldn't give her another tummy tuck. I was standing in the kitchen doorway as they went at it the way they always did. She was throwing pots and pans and he was grabbing her and pushing her. I think I shouted out because my parents turned to the door and my mother roared at me to get out because her sagging figure was all my fault anyway. Only her words weren't that restrained. Neither was their fight.'

But he didn't want to scare Archie away. To make her fear that he was *too* damaged.

'Kaspar!' Her cry tugged at something he couldn't identify. 'How old were you?'

'Who knows?' He shrugged. 'It wouldn't have been a unique occurrence. I ran for the phone, I don't know who I was going to call. Anybody, I guess. Then I recall his footsteps thundering behind me, cuffing me across the back of the head and telling me to mind my own business. Then he picked me up, opened the front door and threw me outside, telling me to go and play in the garden or the sandpit or something. Only no one was as polite as that.'

He had a hundred memories like that locked away in some dark, deep pit of his mind. In many of them he'd copped a lot more of the blame, verbally and physically.

'Didn't anybody know?'

'There was a woman who lived down the road. Her husband was some high-flying guy in the city. She'd been the stay-at-home wife, and also his punch-bag. Her kids had grown up and moved out and she took me in often enough, gave me milk and a cookie. Somewhere to lick my wounds. She made me feel cared for. Like

I wasn't alone.' He shrugged again, not able to put into words how much she had helped him, in her own way.

'That's appalling,' Archie uttered in disbelief. 'I never really understood.'

'Why would you? Your childhood was so different. And that can only be a good thing.'

She shook her head at him.

'How can you be so blasé?'

Kaspar wasn't sure how to answer that. 'I don't know. It was just…how things were. It was normal to me. It could have been worse, I guess. A lot of the time they didn't really take much notice of me at all. If I stayed out of their way I could pretend the shouting and screaming and fighting was some bad movie on a TV in another room. I used to pretend I was somewhere else. Someone else.'

'Is that why you used to love school so much? Because it made it easier to pretend?'

'I guess. I never really thought about it.' Actually, that wasn't true. He'd thought about it from time to time. 'I don't think it was personal, Archie, as odd as you might think that sounds. I don't think it was ever about me. It was always about them. That was the point.'

'Is that what you think?' She shook her head.

'I guess. It's what your father once said to me.'

'I remember Dad used to take us into his workshop and help us make a wooden toy, or later a metal one on his lathe, and weave long stories that you couldn't help but find yourself caught up in.' Archie laughed softly. 'The next thing you'd be pouring your heart out to him about whatever was wrong. At least, *I* would be.'

He smiled, bowing his head so that she couldn't read his expression. He suspected it was suddenly a fraction too wistful. Of all the people he'd felt he'd let down when he'd lost his cool that night in the bar, it was Archie's father. To this day, he had no idea whether the man ever knew about the monumental mistake he'd made that night.

Suddenly Kaspar felt too full of sorrow for all he had lost over the years but never previously allowed himself to mourn. He swallowed, breathed, waiting until he felt less emotional.

Him. Emotional?

'Your father helped me to realise that it wasn't my fault. Whatever they said there was nothing that I did or didn't do that influenced them. I was an easy target, but they would have followed the same path with each other whether I'd been around or not.'

'You sound so…rational about it all.' A hint of wonderment coloured her tone. 'So logical. I can't imagine how I could handle it the way you do.'

A laugh escaped him. A hollow, empty sound that seemed to bounce off every hard, flat surface.

'You have no idea. I don't handle it, Archie. I never have. I ignore it, hiding it away somewhere and pretending it doesn't exist. I did it successfully for years, but in the end it all bubbled over. I physically hurt someone, Archie. Why do you think I've let the press portray me as this ridiculous "Surgeon Prince of Persia"? Because it's what I deserve.'

'You don't deserve anything of the sort.'

'Yes. I do. Why do you think I avoid relationships? Why do you think I avoid emotional connections of any kind? Why do you think that until you came along I didn't want to settle down and have a family of my own? I couldn't bear the idea that I might do to them even a fraction of what was done to me.'

'You could never do that,' Archie asserted fiercely, the certainty in her voice surprising him as much as it warmed him. 'You aren't them. You're nothing like them.'

'I was never sure of that before. Not until you turned up, carrying my child. Not until that moment when I knew I *would* be a part of my baby's life. A full, complete part, not some part-time dad. I won't accept that, Archie. And I won't let you relegate me to that. That's why we had to marry.'

He couldn't tell her that he was becoming more and more suspicious that it was only part of it.

She watched him intently, her eyes never leaving his face.

'And what about love?' she challenged, so quietly he had to strain to hear her.

There was no reason for his heart to suddenly hang a beat. He didn't like what it might mean. What it might be trying to tell him. Kaspar forced himself to regain control.

'I can't tell you about love,' he informed her steadily. 'But I can tell you about chemistry.'

'Five months ago?' She let out a nervous laugh.

'It wasn't just that night, Archie. You know it as well as I do. That kiss before proves it.'

She wanted to argue. But she didn't. She couldn't. And he felt that was a good start.

She was still riding on the unexpected high of Kaspar opening up to her the following day when they were back in Dr Jarvis's office. Wondering if marriage to Kaspar would be so bad after all. Her marriage to Joe might have gone wrong, but they hadn't had a fraction of the chemistry Kaspar had mentioned. Not to mention the fact that she was carrying Kaspar's baby.

Could it really be that easy? Fitting together so neatly? It almost felt too good to be true.

'Right.' Dr Jarvis strode across the room to them, snagging Archie's attention as she advanced.

The woman's expression was too careful. Something dark, and terrifying, churned inside her.

'So I've spoken to your doctor and got your records, as you know, and I've carried out another examination today. I believe that there is funnelling taking place. However, it's no more advanced than when I examined you last week.'

Kaspar's arm unexpectedly moved around her back, and instinctively she leaned into it, drawing strength from his solid body.

'So what happens next?' he asked clearly, calmly, like he knew her vocal cords were too paralysed to even try to speak.

He probably knew already, of course. He was asking for her benefit. But that only made her all the more grateful.

'It means it's your call, Archana. There's no need to become alarmed but, given your history I would be prepared to do a cerclage in the expectation that it might help to ensure this baby stays in there where it needs to be.'

'What would that entail?' She swallowed a wave of nausea, trying to focus, to understand.

'I would place a band of strong thread around the neck of your womb, under spinal anaesthetic. I could do it this afternoon and it should take around twenty-five minutes. Antibiotics will help to reduce the risk of infection but I would want to keep you in for at least twenty-four hours anyway to ensure that the procedure hadn't induced labour. After that you should be able to go home provided you take things very easy.'

'Bed rest?' Kaspar sounded gravelly compared to his usual voice, but Archie couldn't process it. She didn't know what it meant.

'For a few days if possible.' Dr Jarvis nodded. 'Then you can slowly start to resume light movements, graduating to normal. With some emergency cerclage, we recommend no sexual intercourse for the duration of the pregnancy, but with Archana the funnelling is so faint that I'm anticipating you can resume sex in a week or two as long as it's light and infrequent, say once or twice a week.'

Later, much later, she would flush at the memory at the rather one-way conversation, and the fact that neither she nor Kaspar had refuted the idea that they were enjoying a healthy sexual relationship.

Later. Not now.

'But you should wear a condom, Kaspar,' Dr Jarvis was continuing blithely. 'Obviously that's more about reducing the risk of infection rather than concern about conception.'

On some vague level Archie was aware that the woman had been making a joke. No doubt one she made to all her patients to try to elevate the mood a fraction. But Archie couldn't laugh, she barely even cracked a smile. She wasn't sure if Kaspar did any better.

'We won't be having sex,' came Kaspar's tight, rasping admission eventually. But when Dr Jarvis continued, it wasn't clear if she had misunderstood or was simply being discreet.

'That's probably wise until I have chance to do a two-week post-op check-up. Then I'll have a better idea of how your body is reacting to the cerclage, Archana. Often orgasms can soften the already compromised cervix, which can also lead to premature birth. Although, again, in your case, I don't believe that will be the case. This is more a precaution due to your history along with the fact that there is faint funnelling. If it was just one of those factors then I wouldn't be considering the procedure.'

And if Kaspar hadn't been the one pulling the strings, would anyone have done anything at all? Her doctors had dismissed it, if they'd even noticed it, just as they had done when she'd been carrying Faith.

She couldn't lose another baby. She *wouldn't*.

She didn't need to look at Kaspar to know what she wanted to do. Somehow, him just being here, his arm around her, gave her the confidence she needed to make her own decision.

'Schedule the procedure, please.' Her voice cracked but she didn't care. 'I'll have it done as soon as possible.'

CHAPTER NINE

THE SUN BEAT DOWN, seeping into Archie's skin and melting into her very bones, its warmth heating the poolside paving slabs under her feet. Archie relaxed in the shade and tried not to stare too obviously at the sight of Kaspar cutting through the water as he executed perfect length after perfect length.

The past few weeks since the cerclage had seemed surreal. Like she'd woken up in a parallel life where she lived in pleasant domesticity with Kaspar. He'd been attentive, and patient, and easy company.

But they'd never mentioned his childhood again. Or their marriage.

They never really talked about anything of substance. Not even the cerclage. Their conversations were light, sometimes funny, always friendly, but they verged on the superficial, and it galled Archie more than she cared to admit.

As though their moment of breakthrough had never happened.

Even when Dr Jarvis had expressed her satisfaction that Archie's body seemed to have accepted the intervention well with bed rest slipping into house rest then into gentle activities, but not yet sexual activity.

Archie had no doubt that her searing cheeks had raised the temperature of the consultation room by several degrees, mortified that she'd instantly thought back to that weekend together and had not been able to get the incredible X-rated images from her head. Yet Kaspar had schooled his features as though the conversation hadn't bothered him in the least.

It had somehow felt demoralising, making her wonder why he hadn't even touched her since the kiss that wedding night. Had it simply been about proving a point? Why did it even bother her?

Archie stood up abruptly. The need to get away from the house—something she hadn't been able to do in the last few days—more overwhelming than ever.

That one moment of openness, of almost vulnerability on Kaspar's part those weeks ago had been gone even by the following morning when she'd awoken. She could remember it as vividly as if it had only been hours ago.

Not even a trace of their temporary connection had remained as he'd presented her with a freshly squeezed orange juice courtesy of the juice-maker on his sparkling kitchen island, scrambled eggs with asparagus on wholemeal toast courtesy of the pan on the pristine cooker, and rich herbal tea courtesy of the instant hot-water tap at the plush sink.

She had plastered a beatific smile to her lips and pretended not to notice that the vulnerable Kaspar had disappeared as abruptly as he'd appeared. Pretended not to care that he hadn't dipped his head and kissed her the way she'd so ardently wished he would as they'd stood in that room, her hand over his heart, trying to feel whether it was beating as loudly and as quickly as hers had been.

But he'd remained as shut off to her as he always had been. A closed book.

'So you do actually use this kitchen for cooking?' It had been an effort to keep her tone upbeat at first. To tease him. 'I'm impressed.'

'You should be. It was your father who taught me how.'

'His only real signature was all-day breakfasts,' Archie had corrected him, this time striving for a laugh. Surprised when it was actually more genuine than she'd expected. 'He was useless at most other cooking.'

'You're right.' Kaspar had nodded after a moment's consideration. 'I've been making his famous all-day breakfast since I was fourteen.'

'Ah, yes. You and Robbie would cook it every single Sunday of every single holiday.'

'I seem to remember you wolfing it down as fast as anybody.'

'I had to.' Archie had feigned indignation. 'I had to keep up with you two. You didn't exactly want a twelve-year-old following you around. You both always tried to ditch me.'

'Yeah.' Kaspar had chuckled. 'And you've no idea the rollicking your father gave us whenever we were successful.'

They'd laughed and, for a moment, it had felt good again. Until she'd realised that all Kaspar's light-hearted banter was a way of keeping her at arm's length. Even as she lived in his home as his wife, carrying his child.

Shaking off her thoughts as she reached the expansive glass sliders that led from the poolside to the cool lounge, Archie sensed, rather than saw, Kaspar coming up behind her as she entered the house.

'Archie? Is everything okay?'

She wanted to shout and rail and vent all her frustrations. Instead, she simply turned to greet him with a pleasant, if rather flat smile plastered onto her lips.

She should be grateful he cared.

She should be.

'I'm fine. The baby's fine. I just wanted to head in for a while.'

He didn't believe her for a moment. His gaze pierced through her, making her blood fizz in her veins in a way that even the hot sun hadn't managed.

Dammit, when was she ever going to get a grip of herself around this man?

'What's wrong?' he demanded. 'You've been more and more jittery with each passing day.'

Fear that he could read her so easily, that he might guess the embarrassing truth, lent her voice a frustration she hadn't intended.

'I'm sick of being cooped up in this house, unable to even go out, when you refuse to talk to me about anything remotely important. I can't take it any more. I'm getting my trainers and I'm going for a walk along the beach.'

He eyed her again, the same intensity, the same knowing expression in those unfathomable depths. How was it that he seemed to find it so easy to read her while she had no idea what he was thinking, most of the time? It was hardly fair.

And now she sounded like the kind of petulant teen she liked to pride herself that she'd never been.

'Have I upset you in some way, Archie?' Evenly. A little too calmly.

'No.' She gritted her teeth.

'Have I treated you badly and not been aware of it?'

'Of course not.'

'Then perhaps you would care to tell me why I suddenly seem to have become your enemy.' His eyebrows shot up. 'Only here was I thinking I was looking after you.'

He had been. That was the problem. He was looking after her for the baby, which was right and proper, but not because he also wanted to look after *her*. The difference was subtle, but it was there. And it hurt.

Logic, it seemed, stood little chance against a heart that yearned for something else. Especially when that something else was Kaspar Athari's love.

Archie balked at the realisation.

Surely she wasn't still imagining herself *in love* with Kaspar? No, that had to be the baby mushing up her head.

'You're right.' She backed down abruptly. 'Sorry. Maybe I just need to get out of the sun.'

The last thing she needed right now was to engage in a bit of verbal back and forth with him. Or stir up more emotions in her that her hormone-riddled head might mistake for *love*. It was all she could manage not to squirm beneath his unrelenting gaze. Assessing her, as he always did.

'Get changed,' he bit out unexpectedly. 'I'm taking you out for the afternoon.'

Flitting around the city, playing the tourist with Archie and doing the sightseeing thing was certainly not the way he'd been expecting this day to turn out. Yet here they were in downtown Los Angeles, soaking up the atmosphere.

To his surprise, he found himself enjoying it, even forgetting his concerns for Archie, and for their baby, for a while.

Over the last week he'd become more and

more aware of the beatific yet simultaneously false smile that she'd flashed him from time to time. He was aware that, to a greater extent, it was his own fault. After opening up to her that one night he'd not so much regretted it but, more, had had his misgivings. At loading something like that onto Archie when she already had enough to worry about. And, yes, about opening up so easily, so naturally. As if it hadn't been the greatest secret he'd lugged around for his entire life, which had defined him, driven him, moulded him. And as though it didn't even matter any more. Not when he had Archie.

Because the truth was, he didn't have Archie. She may have married him, but only because she'd been pregnant with his baby and he'd insisted on it. He would do well to remember that before he risked letting himself get carried away with this sham marriage of theirs. The marriage he was altogether too happy to accept. So he'd managed to shut himself off to her as he always had. A closed book.

But always aware that Archie could so easily take him off the shelf, blow the cobwebs away and open him up if she took it into her head. Encouraging him to give up his stories, his secrets when they were better left unread.

Unseen.

'The Walt Disney Concert Hall?' she breathed, a look of quiet awe on her face as she dragged him back to the present.

'Yeah, well, I figured with your background in construction this might be of particular interest.'

'It is.' Archie nodded, taking in the iconic structure in front of them. 'The way it looks and, I believe, the sound are incredible.'

He dipped his head in confirmation.

'The LA Philharmonic are performing next month. I have tickets. Accompany me.'

It was meant to be an invitation but he knew it sounded more like a command. Even more unexpectedly, however, Archie merely looked up at him in surprise and then smiled. A genuine, sweet smile that he felt everywhere, as if she were running her hands over his bare flesh the way he knew her eyes had been doing—albeit against her will—earlier in the afternoon at the pool.

She made him feel so good. Perhaps too good. He didn't have any right to still want her the way he did. As wrong as he knew it was—she was the mother of his child, after all, and he was supposed to be caring for her, protecting her—he couldn't seem to stop it. She preyed on his waking thoughts. And most definitely his sleeping thoughts.

'Come on.' He forced one leg in front of the other, but his hand still reached for hers as he led her around the building he'd somehow *known* she would love to see.

The tour should have been a welcome distraction, allowing him to clear his head, but Kaspar was too preoccupied to enjoy it. He was just grateful that Archie seemed happy, throwing herself into the history and the story as though nothing was more important to her.

After that, they toured the MAK Center for Art and Architecture, the gardens at the exposition centre and another museum whose name he couldn't remember afterwards. Yet each time she barely seemed to notice he was even accompanying her while, for Kaspar, the drive in the back of the chauffeured car was becoming a little harder with each journey. He couldn't shake an irrational urge to jolt her, to remind her that he wasn't just the guy who'd got her pregnant, he was her husband. Whatever that meant.

'Where now?' Archie asked as she glanced out the window as if she had any idea where they were.

'Home.'

It was ridiculous how those words rippled through him, but it was only when Archie shivered that he realised she wasn't quite as immune to him as he'd let himself believe. With mounting curiosity he watched her force herself not to react, grasping instead at the first thing to come into her head.

'You mean that incredible house you own with the stunning views? Though I couldn't describe it as a *home.*'

'By which you mean…?' he prompted when she stopped talking with a strangled sound.

'Forget I said anything.'

He knew he should do precisely that. Let it go. It wouldn't do any good to encourage the kind of conversation they'd had the other night. Yet he couldn't just stay silent. He wanted to know what she thought. It *mattered* to him.

He didn't care how dangerous that sounded. At least it was something more than the trivial conversations they'd been having recently. He told himself he was being foolish. But *that* didn't seem to matter at all.

For her part, despite all the biting of her lip, which he was fast recalling meant that Archie was trying to bite back words she knew she shouldn't say, Archie swivelled her head to look at him.

'It's hardly a home, Kaspar. It doesn't have an ounce of heart. It doesn't tell a visitor the slightest thing about the person who owns it. It's a beautiful building but it's soulless. There's nothing of *you* in it.'

She was right, of course. Because that was exactly how he'd wanted it. At some point he'd come to equate being unreadable with being invulnerable. Not that he would ever have admitted that before now, of course.

'So change it.' He shrugged as though it was no big deal but his eyes never left hers.

As if somehow that way he could convey all the thing he couldn't, *shouldn't*, say. He told himself it was part of the plan. A necessity. To break down the barriers in order that they could grow close enough to be the kind of parents their child would need. It wasn't about *wanting* to break down barriers with Archie.

He wasn't sure even he believed himself.

What the hell was wrong with him?

'Sorry? Change what?' she pushed tentatively.

'Change the house.' He waved a hand that he was glad to see didn't look as leaden as it felt. 'We're married and we're having a baby. That place is your house too now, so make it a home. The family home of your dreams.'

'What, to match the marriage of my dreams? I can change anything, but without your input it will just be *my* home in *your* house. It still won't reflect you at all.'

The tone verged on hysterical. Out of no-where, or so it felt. The words cracked out like a whip slicing through the air. He had to fight not to flinch.

'So?' he replied coldly, not trusting himself to say any more.

The silence was so stark that he could hear the almost silent hum of tyres on tarmac. Archie blew out a deep breath.

'I just don't understand you, Kaspar.' She splayed her hands out on her knees. 'It's like we take one step forward only to take a giant leap back.'

'I disagree.'

'Really? One minute you're telling me we won't be playing happy families, the next you're hauling me off to the registrar. You kiss me like we're in some kind of epic movie, but then you don't even look sideways at me. You open up to me finally about something that actually *matters*, and then you shut me out as though I have no right to know anything about you. Now you're telling me we can redecorate your house like a real couple but you barely react when I challenge you about this not being a real marriage. Which version of *Kaspar* should I believe in?'

'The movie version sounds good. This is Hollywood after all.' He didn't know how he managed to sound appropriately dry. Even amused. 'This place loves a good "Girl Next Door Tames Playboy" love story after all.'

'This isn't a movie,' she snapped, a little shakily. 'This is my life.'

'Now it's both.'

She exhaled again. Even deeper this time, and more forcefully.

'If this really were a movie, Kaspar, you wouldn't be shutting me out.'

He really didn't like the way his blood suddenly rushed through his body at her accusation.

'I haven't shut you out,' he managed, although

even on his lips the words sounded hollow. 'I opened up to you.'

'One conversation? One night?' She was incredulous. 'That's your idea of opening up? You cracked the portcullis a fraction and then the next morning you'd not only slammed it back down but you'd dug a moat, filled it and set me squarely on the other side.'

His jaw locked so tightly he thought his bones might crack, but he couldn't refute her accusation. More to the point, *why did he find he even wanted to*?

'What did you expect me to do?' he demanded. 'Rage and roar and gnash my teeth? That isn't who I am, Archie. I thought you knew that.'

She flinched, just as he'd expected she would. But then she rallied. Quickly.

'I didn't expect you to treat me like the enemy because you regretted even that tiny show of vulnerability from yourself. I didn't expect you to push me even further away. I didn't expect you to shoot down any conversations that involved anything real.'

'You saw a bike with stabilisers in a shop and asked what colour we would for buy our baby,' he stated in disbelief. 'The baby isn't even born yet.'

'It was hypothetical. And it wasn't just that. It was about getting an opinion from you on anything at all. You know exactly what I mean. Every conversation. Every time.'

He shot her a deliberately disparaging look.

'I don't know anything of the sort. You're being overly dramatic.'

He did know, though. That was the issue. For a moment she didn't answer, but when she did it wasn't to say what he might have expected.

'Please, Kaspar. I know you *do* understand.'

Her soft plea scraped away inside him. Raw. Guilt-inducing. He tried to ignore it. Turned his head to watch the LA landscape as it sped past the window, the sights and smells as clear to him as if he'd been able to taste then, feel them, without the thick glass and metal in the way.

Abruptly he hit the intercom, instructing his driver to change direction.

'What's Hector's?' Archie asked, despite herself, and, incredibly, a smile began toying with his lips.

How did she change the mood so easily? Bring him around when he'd thought things too dour?

'You'll see,' he replied, only half-surprised when the hint of teasing didn't satisfy her. 'Fine, it's a crazy golf course. I used to go there all the time when we first moved out here and I was sixteen.'

She eyed him, a little too knowingly.

'Do you remember the course we used to sneak onto as kids? When it was closed for the day and the guy who ran it knew we didn't have enough pocket money to pay full price but he let us give him whatever money we could scrape together?'

'And then he'd leave us whatever pastries hadn't been sold that day and were going to get chucked out anyway?' Kaspar added.

Archie laughed, her face flushing with pleasure.

'You were really good at crazy golf. Robbie used to hate it because sometimes you'd hit the shots backwards just to give him a chance.'

'Considering how co-ordinated he was at other sports, he really was remarkably bad at the game. So were you, for that matter. The athletic Coates kids, foiled by a crazy golf course.'

'I wasn't that bad,' she objected.

'You weren't that good either.'

'Now wait a minute...' She paused, then

jabbed her finger at the tinted glass with barely disguised delight. 'There. Is that Hector's?'

He knew the drive without even looking.

'That's Hector's.'

'Come on, then.' She was out of the door the minute the car pulled up. 'I reckon today might be the day for a little payback.'

He vaulted after her.

'Payback, huh? Care to wager?'

'How much?'

'Not money. A forfeit.'

She wrinkled her nose.

'What kind of forfeit?'

'Winner gets to choose.' He shrugged, striding ahead and slapping the money on the counter of a rather disinterested-looking young man.

'Surely that's not Hector?' Archie whispered as they ducked through the paint-chipped turnstile.

He wasn't fooled.

'Changing the subject, Coates. Are you that doubtful about your crazy golf abilities?'

'I am not.' She selected her club and thrust her chin in the air. 'Fine. A forfeit. Winner's choice.'

In the event, the game was more fun than he had anticipated. Light relief after the tension.

He'd never thought that revisiting any element of his past could ever be anything but painful, but he was beginning to understand that in his need to bury his childhood he had lost many happier times. Almost always concerning the Coates family, the way her father had taught him to be a man, or the way Robbie had shared everything with him, or the way Archie had treated him like another annoying big brother. They had made him feel like any other normal boy. A person, not an *it*.

All too soon, they were at the final obstacle, their game almost over, and Archie hadn't been quite as appalling as he'd remembered.

Still, Kasper knew it was a mistake the moment he moved behind her, her back against his chest, his arms skating down the length of hers, her delicate hands under his, all under the pretext of holding the golf club with her and allowing her to help him make his winning shot.

Until that moment it had been a good game. Simple, uncomplicated fun, a round of crazy golf on a balmy afternoon. They had exchanged banter and laughed and she had teased him, coughing and doing funny dances to try to put him off his shots, like a grown-up version of the Little Ant he had known. Her ploy hadn't worked, his shots had been true each time. But occasionally he'd pretended her antics had put him off, making some melodramatic mishit that had only made her laugh all the more.

A genuine, throw-her-head-back laugh, which was surpassed only by the vivid sparkle in her glorious eyes. The more she did so, the more he yearned to make her do it more. The intense pleasure it gave him to be the person making her so outwardly happy had taken him back, made him forget who or where he was. It seduced him into focussing on Archie and himself together, simply playing crazy golf. Like when they'd been young, carefree, their whole lives ahead of them.

She'd played well but he'd played better. Of course he had. Because everything in life was a competition for him. And yet, right at that moment, he'd wanted them both to take that winning shot. He'd invited her to join him and she, without even thinking about it, had skipped almost girlishly to comply.

The moment his body had touched hers everything changed. The innocence of the moment was gone, replaced instead by something far more charged. Far more sensual. Only then did Kaspar admit it had been there all afternoon. Simmering quietly. Just waiting to catch them unawares.

He should move back. But he couldn't. He could barely even breathe. His head was over her shoulder, his cheek brushing her ear as they both stared at the ball. Archie's own breathing was shallow, fast, although he knew she was trying to fight it, desperately struggling to control it. He could take the shot, pretend he didn't feel what she felt. But he was powerless to move. Rooted where he stood.

He turned his head, so very, very slightly it should have been imperceptible. But Archie noticed. She knew. Her head mirrored his, and now their mouths were an inch apart and the beast inside him was roaring with the compulsion to close the gap. His body wanting her with the same ferocity it had all those months ago.

He had to walk away.

Now.

CHAPTER TEN

KASPAR DROPPED HIS head but misjudged it.
Or rather he judged it perfectly, his lips skimming the bare skin just above the neckline of
her T-shirt. Archie shivered and he was lost.

Before he could think once, let alone twice,
Kaspar tilted his head and then they were kissing as she pressed her back into him, their
hands still holding the grip of the golf club and
his feet still positioned on either side of hers.

He drank her in, her taste, her feel, her scent
every bit as perfect as the recollection imprinted on his brain, and yet also a hundred
times better. He remembered kissing every inch
of her skin, tracing it with his fingertip, his
mouth, his tongue, and as his body tightened
against Archie's perfect bottom, she pushed
back against him, then gentlest of moans reaching his ears.

He almost lost it, there and then. A lifetime
of being in complete control gone because no

one else had ever got under his skin like this. No one but Archie. He would never know how he managed to pull his brain into focus, to remember where they were, or that he was meant to be easing Archie's stress, not adding to it.

It took everything he had to wrench his mouth away. This was pure physical desire, nothing more. *Nothing more*. But if that was true then why was he still behind her, why were his arms still around hers, her hands still held under his?

If he didn't stop now, he wasn't sure he ever would. Somehow he found the strength to pull away.

The loss of contact was almost painful.

'What was that for?' Archie whispered, turning slowly to face him, her fingers hovering over her lips.

He wondered if her mouth burned for him as his did for her.

'Call it my victory kiss.' His attempt to sound casual fell far short of the mark. 'Your forfeit.'

'You didn't win.'

Half teasing, half shaky, and entirely shocked. He knew exactly how she felt.

'You'd better finish the game to prove it.'

'I don't give a damn about the game.'

He just gave a damn about her.

'The game, Athari.' She emitted a delicious growl.

All he really wanted was to haul her back into his arms and finish kissing her, thoroughly and completely. Even though it made absolutely no sense.

'Right,' he muttered eventually, stepping forward and taking the proffered club.

Stepping to the mark, he swung and hit. He barely even waited to see if it reached its mark. He knew it would.

'Let's go.' He spun around and begun walking away, but he couldn't help extending his arm behind him. Felt triumphant when she took his hand without a word.

He told himself it meant nothing, the way his chest constricted as her fingers entwined with his. He promised himself he'd let go as soon as they were back in the car.

But now they were back in the vehicle and he still hadn't let go of her hand. He still couldn't take his gaze off her sparkling eyes as he instructed his driver to finally take them home. He couldn't shake the fact that the word *home* sounded somehow right, and natural, and easy, and perfect.

Archie stared right back at him, her gaze never leaving his for a moment, but he saw the hesitation on her face. Watched the way her tongue flicked out nervously to wet her lips.

'Why are you looking at me like that?'

Uncertainty in her tone mingled with raw need. Kaspar gritted his teeth. It was a heady combination.

'You realise that we kissed out there. Like a proper married couple.'

'Imagine that,' she tried to tease him, but her breathy tone belied her confidence.

Another Archie quality that he apparently found sexy as hell. Especially after the overly cocky women of his past. *What had he ever seen in them?* The answer was clear now. He hadn't. They'd been the perfect choice for a man looking to keep himself emotionally unavailable because they'd never threatened to unravel his carefully crafted design. The construct that Archie had picked apart in a matter of months. Or, indeed, one heady weekend.

'If people see us, recognise me with a woman looking as unambiguously pregnant as you look, your photo will be all over the papers. The internet. We might have kept things out of the media for now, but they will find out eventually and it *will* fire up their interest.'

'So you'll control it.' She schooled her features. But it was too late, he'd seen that flash of contempt in her eyes. 'You control anything you want to. You're Kaspar Athari.'

Until a few months ago he might have believed her.

'Not anything,' he muttered. 'I can't control how I am when I'm with you.'

The words were out before he could swallow them back. Archie paused, as though momentarily unable to answer. Then her hand reached out, slowly, tentatively, giving him plenty of time to draw away. Had he wanted to. Her fingertips brushed his jaw. Gentle. Careful. But it fired him up nonetheless.

Before he could stop himself, he was lifting her through the air to settle her on his lap and her soft, startled cry even as she leaned instinctively into him, her arms slipping around his neck and her bottom nudging against the hottest, hardest part of him, only acted as an accelerant to the fire.

He closed the gap and allowed himself to taste her all over again, light and deep, languid and demanding. Indulging in the feel, the scent, the breathy sounds of pleasure that were so essentially Archie when he plundered her mouth and pressed kisses into the creases at either corner. She quivered deliciously as he scorched a trail down her neck to the sensitive hollow where his lips, his tongue, his teeth all worked in harmony until she was breathing hard and wriggling on his lap. And he was aching, *physically* aching, for her.

His hands found their way to the hem of her T-shirt, hauling it over her head in one fluid movement, and as her hair tumbled back down and over her shoulders, he couldn't help lifting one hand to wind it around his fist, pulling just the wrong side of gently to tilt her mouth back up to his and claim her all over again.

Archie pressed her chest to him. Hard nipples scraped urgently against him, even through his own thin shirt. She fumbled with the buttons, tugging them open and rubbing against him as though the skin-to-skin contact might somehow alleviate her longing. And Kaspar loved it. The way she acted out of pure desire. The feel and the taste, and what she wanted. The kind of women he'd been with before her had been too busy trying to show him how good they were and too hung up on the aesthetics of it.

He let his thumb graze one swollen peak with deliberate nonchalance, moving quickly away when she arched her back in order to repeat the action. She groaned softly.

'Kaspar...'

'What is it, Archie?'

He was amazed that he could managed to sound even a fraction as in control as he did.

'You know what,' she whispered, pushing her chest to his again.

'Tell me,' he rasped. 'I want to hear it.'

She flushed slightly, but met his eyes boldly.

'Touch me.'

It was like some exquisite torture, keeping his hands to himself. But he wanted to hear her say it. He thirsted to hear the longing in her tone, knowing that it was a need only he could sate for her.

For both of them.

'Where?' he demanded.

'Anywhere,' she whispered. 'Everywhere.'

He couldn't stand it any longer. Dropping his head back to the hollow, he kissed and teased.

'Here?'

'There,' she agreed, tilting her head to one side to allow him better access. Taking his time, he made his way down her body, his fingertips hooking down the lace of her bra to free one perfect nipple.

'Here?'

She gasped, and nodded, her head falling back slightly as he licked, sucked. And with every stroke of his tongue he stoked the fire and revelled in the way the flames roared within him. It was all he could do to stay where he was, lavishing attention on first one rosy peak and then the other. Then back again, as her breathing grew ever more shallow, catching in her throat.

And then he was sliding his hand up the bare skin of her thigh, the summery skirt puddling around her bottom as though only too happy to fall away for him. Archie moaned, a low, soft, long sound that seemed to wind its way through him and coil around his sex as potently as if it were her delicate hand. He reached the top of one thigh and then, his knuckles barely brushing her hot, molten core, he skimmed his way slowly down the other thigh.

'You're teasing me again,' she moaned, burying her head in his shoulder.

Half a gasp, half a growl, but wholly frustration. Another shot fired through him.

'I am,' he managed, shocked at how difficult it suddenly seemed to speak.

Kaspar could stand it no longer. He ached for her. Physically *ached.* He wanted her. And she was his. He lifted his hand and slid it beneath the silky triangle of material.

Hot. Wet. So very ready for him.

He had never wanted anything more than he wanted her right now. It was time to claim her. Brand her as his. He would never want anyone the way he wanted Archie.

She froze at exactly the same moment he did.

What the hell was he thinking? She was pregnant. With his baby. And Catherine had said there could potentially be an issue. They couldn't risk it. They couldn't take that chance. Allowing himself to be driven by his desire, his emotion was exactly the kind of selfishness that his parents had exhibited time and again. He would not repeat their mistakes.

He would not let the fact that he shared their DNA make him like them.

'This can't happen,' he growled, lifting her bodily of his lap and placing her as far across the back seat as he possibly could. Never more grateful for the privacy glass which concealed them from both the driver and the outside world.

She made a sound. It might have been a mutter of agreement but he didn't care. He busied himself locating her clothes. Fastening his shirt.

'That should never have started.' He was aware that he was directing the fury he felt at himself towards Archie, but he couldn't seem to stop himself. 'You have the baby to consider.'

What the hell was wrong with him?

'Dr Jarvis said occasional light sex is acceptable,' she parroted. 'It's not as if we're going at it every day.'

A flush raced up her cheek as though she could scarcely believe her own audacity. It was more of a turn-on than he was prepared to admit.

'This can never happen again.' Determined, Kaspar cut her off. 'This *will* never happen again.'

But she was becoming emboldened.

'Really? Because it seems that the more time we spend together, the more it's inevitable.'

For a moment she actually sounded like it wasn't such a bad thing. And he wanted too much to believe her. If he stayed, he was sure that he'd wind up letting her talk him into things when he ought to know better.

'Then it seems clear to me that the only solution is to spend *less* time together.'

'You're going to stay at the hospital,' she guessed, cutting in.

'One of us has to take responsibility for this... *thing* between us.'

To his shock, she swung around, her eyes flashing with a fury he hadn't seen in her since she'd been a little kid shut out of the more daring exploits he and Robbie had egged each other onto.

'That's not taking responsibility, Kaspar. That's running away. It's not something I thought I'd ever see you do.'

It was only when the car pulled into the drive of Kaspar's oceanside home that Archie felt she could finally breathe again, let alone speak. Ever since her uncontrolled outburst the atmosphere in the car had pulsed with barely suppressed fury, but Kaspar hadn't uttered a word to her.

If he had, she feared she might have melted from their molten ire. The urge to run inside and bolt the door was almost overwhelming, but if she did that then Kaspar would leave. She didn't want him to.

So instead she folded her arms across her chest and summoned one last ounce of strength.

'Don't go, Kaspar. Not tonight.'

For a moment she thought he was going to ignore her, but then he turned his head, his eyes pinning her to the seat.

'I have to.'

'Please.' She couldn't say what passed between them, or what it meant, but she knew instinctively that he was going to stay. 'Take me for a walk along the beach?'

Carefully, with his arm under her elbow, she made her way down the hillside to the beach, slipping her sandals off and spreading her toes in the soft sand. She tilted her face towards the warm setting sun and realised that in spite of everything she wasn't unhappy, or lonely, or wishing she'd never got on that damned plane to America.

To Kaspar.

Because if she hadn't got on that plane then she wouldn't be here now, walking along the beach and realising that even if he never loved her the way she wanted him to, he would always love their child. Always fight for him or her.

'Why are you so determined to fight your feelings for me, Kaspar? Whatever they amount to. This isn't just about the risk to the baby, is it? You're scared to let go with me. Why?'

'It's for your benefit,' he bit out.

'What is it you think I need protecting from? You? In case you've forgotten, I know the other side of you. That kid who I think is more of the real you than you've ever allowed anyone else to see. A good, kind kid.'

'Then your memory isn't what you think is,' he mocked derisively.

'It's exactly what I think it is. Why haven't you met someone before now, Kaspar? Had a family? You really will make a strong, good, supportive father.'

It took a little while for him to answer and, for several long moments, she wondered if he was ever going to answer her.

'My mother is, in polite terms, an oxygen thief,' he stated. 'She always has been. My father was no better. So what does that make me? Their son. Their blood. The lethal mix of the worst of the both of them.'

'I've said it before—you aren't like them, Kaspar.'

'You don't know what I really am like.'

'Maybe, but I don't think you do either.'

It was a silent challenge and he could either ignore her or talk to her. She knew what she wanted him to do, but she tried not to let herself get too carried away.

'I…don't *do* emotion, Archie,' he managed, at length. 'I don't connect with people. I'm not built that way. I know how destructive so-called relationships might be. How intense and violent and toxic. You say I'm not like them, but I'm still a product of them. I share their DNA and even if it wasn't about nature, I was certainly around them long enough for it to be nurture.'

'Is that why you've made a point, all these years, of never allowing yourself to get caught up with any one woman?'

'It's easier that way.'

'It's lonely,' she refuted. 'And it doesn't suit you. You're a decent guy, underneath all the playboy rubbish.'

'Did you know that as a teenager I stole a girl from under Robbie's nose? Not because I liked her or particularly wanted to date her but because Robbie did and I didn't want him ditching me to spend time to with her. That was when I realised I wasn't rounded and *normal*. I wasn't the decent human being your father tried to teach me to be. I was a product of my own parents, already on the way to becoming damaged and twisted.'

'You can't be serious.' Archie swing around to gawk at him. '*That's* what you're basing part of your argument on? *Shady Sadie?* Because I can tell you plenty of mean things my brother and I did to each other and so-called friends as we were growing up. It's called a part of being a kid. And a teenager who thinks the world revolves around them.'

'No, Archie. It's not just that. You don't want to know the things I did when I came out here. They weren't part of growing up, they were out of control. Harmful.'

His face twisted painfully but she couldn't believe it. Not of Kaspar.

'You mean after your mother dragged you out here? Ripped you away from the tiniest bit of security you'd ever had? You played up? But look at you now. You turned your back on the Hollywood scene she'd mapped out for you and instead became a skilled surgeon, a decent person. You volunteer your time to make surgical trips to war zones to help people who really need you.'

He looked frustrated, and angry, and drained. But most of all he looked torn. She'd never seen him look that way before. Her whole body ached for him.

'It's not as altruistic as you think. Did you ever stop to wonder why I went from acting to surgery? Did you think that out of nowhere I developed a driving need to take after my volatile, unpredictable plastic surgeon father?'

'Becoming a surgeon like him doesn't also make you as…unhinged as him,' she cried.

'That's where you're wrong. I'm every bit as out of control as he was. That's *exactly* why I turned my back on acting and suddenly worked to get into a good school, gain a good degree, get into med school.'

'You got into top universities, Kaspar. Not just good schools.'

'You're missing the point. I wasn't doing it because I was a good person, I did it because it was the only way I could think of to make amends for…something I did. So bad that even you couldn't make excuses for me if you knew, Archie.'

'Isn't that the definition of *good*? How long are you going to punish yourself, though?' she whispered. 'What did you do that was so bad?'

The quiet was almost oppressive.

'I fought someone, Archie. I put them in hospital because they looked at me the wrong way in a bar one night.'

Her chest stretched and ached. So that was how that story Katie had told her that night at the charity wrap party had got started. Still, she knew there had to be more to it than that.

'How old were you?'

'Old enough to know better.'

'How old?' she demanded.

'Seventeen.'

'And the other guy?'

'Twenty-five, though I didn't know that at the time. I saw them in court.'

Her stomach lifted and dropped.

'Them?'

'There was another lad.' Kaspar lifted his shoulders. 'But he was almost too drunk to walk. He'd just been swinging a piece of wood around.'

'A piece of wood in a bar? And no one did anything?'

'We were outside by then, in a back alley.'

'And all because they looked at you the wrong way? I don't understand.'

Kaspar gritted his teeth, obviously hating every moment of the story but determined to tell her, to make her understand why he was so *damaged*.

'We were in a bar, a bit of a dive. As they passed me, one of them tripped over my bar stool. He pushed me off it and told me to apologise. I refused and they suggested taking it outside and I didn't have the sense to say no.'

'So there were two of them and one of them was wielding a plank of wood. My God, Kaspar, you could have been killed. Surely you were just defending yourself?'

'No, I wasn't drunk. They were. I could have walked away. I should have.'

'You were seventeen,' she cried. 'It was a mistake.'

'I hospitalised the guy. They were both swinging at me and I saw red. I made a kick—*one* kick, Archie—and I broke his jaw. He needed reconstructive surgery.'

'God, Kaspar.' Her fingers were pressed to her mouth.

'In one stupid, drunken, angry moment I'd changed some stranger's life.'

'It…it was one kick, Kaspar.'

'Exactly. What if I'd really lost control and not been able to stop even there?'

For a moment she couldn't respond and then, suddenly, it was easy.

'But you *didn't* lose control. You stopped. One kick, unfortunately well placed but hardly premeditated or unprovoked. What did the judge say?'

'It doesn't matter what he said. It's what I know that counts.'

'So he said it was self-defence?' she guessed.

'The guy was wasted, he probably couldn't have hurt me, but still the judge dismissed the case,' Kaspar said contemptuously.

'Because even a drunken guy could get lucky if he'd, say, picked up a bar stool, or a glass ashtray, or who knows what else,' she argued. 'What did the judge say?'

He eyed her reluctantly.

'That there were too many witnesses who had told him how those men were acting up all night, were always in there, acting that way. He said *I* was the innocent party and he let me walk away scot-free.'

'Only you didn't walk away scot-free, did you? You changed your whole life because of that one incident. Your whole new career choice was based on that moment, wasn't it? Because of the surgeons who repaired that lad's face? They're who you wanted to become?'

'It was a hell of a lot better than the out-of-touch, diva-like actor that I was becoming.'

'It was self-sacrificing.'

'Hardly,' he snorted. 'I knew if I turned my back on the lucrative deal my mother had just made with a major studio, she'd never forgive me. Two birds, one stone.'

It was pointless arguing. She knew the truth and she felt sure Kaspar did, too, deep down. Instead, she reached her hand out, placing her palm on his chest, feeling the heat and thrumming of his heartbeat.

Drawing strength from it.

'You didn't just become an average doctor, Kaspar, you became one of the top surgeons in the world. A pioneer in your field. You're even more famous than some of Hollywood's best A-listers. And what's more, you save lives. Do you really believe you're still damaged? Out of control? Just like your parents?'

'It isn't what I believe, Archie,' he bit out, remorse etched into every contour of his face. 'It's what I know.'

'You're wrong.' She shook her head vigorously but she already knew Kaspar wasn't listening.

She'd lost him. Again.

CHAPTER ELEVEN

'THIRTY-TWO WEEKS.' CATHERINE, as Archie had finally come to know her, smiled as she finished up the examination. 'And you're doing really well.'

'The cerclage is okay?'

'It's fine. If anything, it appears to have lengthened the cervix and reversed the funnelling that we were seeing before. It's a great sign but it can be temporary so don't think it's a green light to start running marathons or anything.'

'So I keep limiting the physical activity.' Archie nodded. 'Got it.'

'And I understand it must be difficult, but you're keeping the sexual activity gentle and less frequent? No more than a couple of times a week?'

She nodded, but couldn't bring herself to look at Kaspar, her face feeling like it probably resembled some kid's rosy-cheeked doll. They'd both agreed it would raise fewer questions if they didn't try to explain the situtation.

'Again, use protection,' Catherine continued blithely. 'More to reduce risk of infection than as contraception.'

Archie forced a laugh. The same joke as last time and just as awkward.

'So now that we're getting closer to the due date—' it felt incredible good saying that '—what can I expect?'

Catherine glanced at Kaspar as if assessing how much he might have told the concerned mum-to-be, then continued professionally as if Archie were any other patient and not one with a renowned OMS sitting next to her.

'If your baby was born right now, barring any health troubles in the womb, it would have a very good chance of surviving and of continuing life with no long-term health problems. One of the most common concerns would be under-development of the respiratory system.'

'Which is one of the reasons we previously considered steroid injections?' Archie prompted.

'Right. However, your body seemed to have been adjusting well to the cerclage so we decided not to go ahead. I think that decision has proved correct given how good it all looks now.'

'So if I go into labour now?'

'If you go into labour now we would still try progesterone or pessaries to try to delay the birth. Every additional day the baby is in there now, he or she is gaining that all-important weight and strengthening internal systems. But as I say, birth at thirty-two weeks has a very good survival rate. Depending on the baby, he or she may spend as little as a week in NICU if feeding and breathing are going OK.'

'And if he can't?'

'If he or she can't—' Catherine's continued care not to give the gender away continued to delight Archie '—then he or she will remain in the NICU with a feeding tube and a respirator for as many weeks or even months as might be necessary. But we'll cross that bridge if and when we come to it.'

'Right.' Archie nodded, her eyes sliding across to Kaspar, who looked remarkably stiff in his chair. She couldn't stop a smile. *Expectant father* mode, not *skilled surgeon* mode. It was so very endearing. She might even say he looked…*content*.

'There's a medical charity event this weekend...' she began, as Catherine nodded in recognition.

'Kaspar's the patron, I know. You want to know if I recommend going?'

'Yes.'

'I don't see why not, depending on how you feel on the day. As long as you take it easy, aren't planning on running around madly getting ready or dancing a jive.'

'Definitely not.' Archie laughed, although maybe it was time for her to show Kaspar a flash of the old, confident Archie.

The one she'd felt returning over recent months. Thanks, ironically, to Kaspar. She'd spent so many years putting him on a pedestal and thinking, somehow, that his lack of interest in her had been because she wasn't pretty, feminine, sexy enough. Especially given Shady Sadie's maturing fifteen-year-old body compared to her thirteen-year-old one. But from that first charity wrap party when he'd homed in on her to the golf course the other day when he hadn't been able to keep from kissing her, Archie was beginning to realise that she had more allure, more dynamism, more *power* than she'd realised.

If Kaspar could resist her then perhaps it was simply because she wasn't trying hard enough to be his undoing. And that sounded like the kind of fun challenge she was more than willing to take up. Perhaps tonight she could remind him what he was missing. That she wasn't just the mother of his baby but a woman in her own right, too.

'Then I'll probably see you there,' said Catherine with a smile.

Archie adopted her most beatific smile, not willing to give Kaspar any forewarning of what was to come.

'I look forward to it.'

Leaning on the bar, an untouched tumbler of some of the most expensive brandy money could buy in hand, Kaspar leaned back against the bar and watched Archie from across the room.

It was a scene that seemed all too familiar to him. An echo of the charity wrap party that had started all of this.

Only this time, instead of having to watch her fend off a couple of admirers on the dance floor and being able to glower in peace, he was forced to pin a smile on his face as she sparkled and floated, as though she was on some kind of mission.

She charmed every single person who stopped to talk to her, particularly the men despite, or perhaps because of, her pregnancy radiance.

And all the while she made sure she was absolutely anywhere but by his side.

It was his own fault, of course. He had no idea what had happened the other day in Catherine's office but Archie had walked out a very different woman. And yet, in many ways, altogether too familiar. More confident, more vivacious, a grown-up version of the Little Ant he'd known. She'd been adamant about accompanying him to this party, and hadn't let any of his, albeit half-hearted, objections deter her.

He was letting her dictate to him. Worse, he was comfortable with it.

To a degree anyway.

Kaspar refused to accept it was because a part of him secretly wanted the world to know the truth. That he was about to become a father. That he, the feckless Surgeon Prince, was quietly content being married to the mother of his baby.

It made no sense.

Archie had even begun to tease him and galled by his constant inability to master his desire around her, he'd determined that tonight he would keep his distance. Allow her to weave her magic of the people in his social circle and the press alike, without his physical presence, which inevitably meant him placing a guarding hand on her here and there. And he knew exactly where that always led to.

Perhaps a part of him had expected her to fail, even hoped she would. Just so that he could finally have a reason to tell himself that this perfect image he'd had of Archie was flawed. That she couldn't possibly be as perfect for him as his mind—and body—seemed to want to believe, and thus she might stop invading his dreams every night. Stop making his body react in ways it had no business reacting when he saw her.

So there she was, working the room and channelling more and more the spirit and boldness he'd begun to remember. And he, for his part, was standing here staring at her like some lovesick puppy.

It would not do.

In a minute he would turn around. He would

find a decent medical conversation and he would throw himself into it, as he always did.

In a minute.

The only thing tempering his immense frustration was that at least the distance afforded him the pleasure of observing, and appreciating, Archie at his leisure. And there was certainly plenty to appreciate in her stunning blue, floor-length ballgown with silver straps that hooked over silky smooth shoulders to cross over beneath her breasts and frame her burgeoning baby bump. Radiant and beautiful. And his.

But she couldn't be.

He could only bring her trouble. His parents' miserable marriage wasn't something he ever wanted to risk inflicting on any woman, but certainly not Archie. And not their child. He had spent too many years terrified, lonely, numb, before he'd met Robbie. Before the Coates family had welcomed him into their safe fold.

They could have seen him as an unwanted entanglement. Yet they had welcomed him. Because he'd wanted to be there. Because he'd craved that life, that stability. And now Archie had returned to him. The fact that she was pregnant with his baby after a one-night stand should have been the greatest unwanted complication of all. Instead, he'd welcomed her. Wanted to be with her. Craved her.

Another man had crossed the room now to greet her, her obvious state of pregnancy apparently not putting him off in the slightest as he leaned in a little too closely to whisper in Archie's ear. *As though the guy didn't care for the fact that Archie was his.* And Archie tipped back her head so that the glorious long line of her elegant neck was exposed, and laughed unashamedly.

Kaspar didn't recall moving from the bar, but suddenly he was across the room in an instant, the blood bubbling and *popping* in his veins. The man didn't even stay long enough to introduce himself, although Kaspar supposed the baring of his teeth in what wouldn't have passed for a smile might have had something to do with it.

'Shall we dance?'

'Are you intending to chase off any male who dares to talk to me, as though you're some dog peeing on a post to mark its territory?' she enquired archly.

He shrugged, unrepentant.

'If I need to.'

'I see.'

Half amusement, half chastisement. Still, Kaspar merely held out his hand. A command rather than a request.

She eyed him, a touch incredulously.

'I'm pregnant.'

'Funnily enough, I hadn't forgotten.'

'Don't be facetious.' She bit her lip. 'I have a bump. The press will photograph us. It will look silly.'

His bump. *His* baby.

'It would never look silly,' he ground out fiercely. 'Besides, isn't this why you insisted we come here tonight? Why else put yourself through this ordeal if not to show the world?'

Without waiting for her to agree, he took her hand and led her to the dance floor. People moved out of their way, one pair of curious eyes after another locking onto them, wondering if this was where he was going to make his unspoken statement to the world. Necks craning to see how his Hollywood royalty mother was taking it.

But he ignored them. No one else mattered anyway. It all simply fell away until there was nothing but the feel of Archie in his arms. At last. Her fingers curled into his, her delicate scent filling his nostrils, their baby cradled in her belly and pressed against him.

They moved together so sinuously, so harmoniously that it felt as though they were melding, just as they had done before. It felt comfortable, and good, and *right*. They danced until the meal was served, a sumptuous feast, which he couldn't remember tasting a morsel of, and some polite, inane conversation that flowed out of his head instantly. He could only remember the feel of Archie's bare skin as his hand rested on her back, or the way she leaned slightly against him, or her hand within his.

And then something changed, so quickly, so suddenly that there was no chance to pre-empt it.

Photographers were crowding in on them, their manner not quite that of the ball's official photographers and Kaspar tensed instinctively. He glanced around, but the security team seemed relaxed and comfortable, and not wanting to make a scene he forced himself to stand down. Ordered himself not to let his imagination, or his worst fears, run riot.

Kaspar had no doubt a hundred cellphones had been capturing them all night, in order to post on the various crude forms of social media so many of the so-called charity supporters favoured. But it didn't bother him.

He only cared about Archie.

And then...

He thrust her back, gently but firmly, shock pulsing through him.

'Was that...?'

'The baby kicking,' she whispered, nodding, her eyes locked onto his as though, like him, she could barely register the other people in around them, the music, the noise.

Tentatively, he reached his arm out and then stopped. Only for Archie to take his hand and place it over her stomach. The kick bounced against him almost immediately. Hard, strong, playful.

Until this point, he'd appreciated everything in the abstract. Whatever other buttons being with Archie had pressed, the baby had always been something he'd known within context. Logically.

Suddenly, there was nothing reasoned or logical about it. Emotions coursed through him and he had absolutely no control over them. But instead of terrifying him, or worrying him, it was almost...*freeing.*

Right up until the throng crowded around them, jostling as they vied for position. Kaspar looked up and saw Archie's face turn from elation to panic. Watched helplessly as she stumbled back a step, a hair's breadth out of his reach so that he couldn't catch her.

And he lost it.

He didn't know what happened next but he had a vague recollection of trying to protect Archie, of grabbing a camera that was so close to her face she squealed and fell back, of it somehow smashing. Not what he'd intended but he didn't care right now. At some point he managed to haul Archie into the safety of his arms. The way her hands clutched at him as though she trusted him, and only him, to protect her, only heightened the wild, savage possessiveness with which he was already fighting a losing battle.

She was his. No one else's. *His.*

He had no idea how he didn't just scoop her into his arms and carry her out of the room. Probably because he knew that might have made her feel undermined and overly fragile, but, still, he recalled bundling her out of the ball and into his car. Throwing himself to the other side of the back seat just so that he didn't give in to this rushing, roaring urge to claim her as his, right there and then in the back of the car.

It was a lethal combination of anger, and fear, and that flicker of helplessness when he'd seen her stumbling and had been unable to get to her in time. Watching it all happen in sickening slow motion. Just like that night when he'd lost control in that back alley fight, doing the only thing that had come into his mind to save himself. Realising too late that if he hadn't been who he was—Kaspar Athari—the thug would probably never have bothered to have a go in the first place.

And if Archie was any other pregnant woman, would the press have crowded in on her like they had? Or was it because of him? Because she was carrying his child?

Kaspar already knew the answer. Of course he did. He should have known better than to risk Archie like this. He should have kept her well away from here.

The car ride couldn't end soon enough. He was out of the door before the vehicle had even come to a stop. Racing around, he snatched open Archie's door and, this time he didn't fight the impulse to lift her into his arms and carry her, still trembling, through the house and to her rooms. Only once he was sure she was settled and okay did he leave, stalking through the corridors until he came to his suite, hauling his clothes over his head, slamming the shower on and stepping inside.

Icy-cold water spilled over his body, biting and unforgiving. But it still couldn't assuage the fire inside him that raged so fiercely it felt as though it was devouring him from the inside out. As it had been all evening, when they'd been so close, so intimate on that dance floor, oblivious to anyone and everyone around them.

There had only been Archie. In perfect, crystal-clear, vibrant detail. Her hand folded into his, her fragile body standing side by side with him. All night. And he had beaten back every single urge to drag her off somewhere more private and haul her onto his lap. Had intended to when he finally got her home.

And then the incident with the photographers had occurred. He'd lost control. Smashed a camera, though he couldn't even remember how. It was all such a blur but it rammed home, in no uncertain terms, that Archie was much better off without him.

And still Kaspar could barely restrain himself from slamming the shower off and pounding down that corridor to Archie's room. Every fibre of his being wanted to drag her back into his arms, lower her onto that bed and drive so deep inside her than he didn't know where he ended and she began.

Pressing his hands to the travertine tiles, Kaspar forced himself to stay where he was, rooting himself to the huge porcelain shower tray. Chill water still coursed off his shoulders, down his chest, his back.

He didn't hear the click of the door but instantly he knew she was in the room. His entire body knew.

Slowly, very slowly, he lifted his head and turned.

She didn't speak but she actually braced herself. The move was almost imperceptible but for the fact that it caused the lapels of her silken nightgown to fall open, exposing the creamy valley of exposed skin and a tantalising glimpse of her breasts, which he'd been imagining kissing, tasting only a few minutes earlier.

It was more than his body could take and as though he was some kind of adolescent kid all over again, Kaspar found his body reacting in the most primitive way it could. He could turn away or he could stand there and ride it out.

His muscles spasmed and clenched as she let her eyes drop down over his body, as surely as if it were her fingers scorching a trail over his skin instead. And then the slight widening of her gaze, the way she sucked in a deep breath, the way her chest swelled that little bit more.

He tightened, so hard it was almost painful. The way only Archie seemed to be able to do to him.

'Stop pushing me away,' she whispered, the longing in her tone twisting inside him worse than any knife or scalpel could have.

'You saw what happened tonight. It's better for you if I keep my distance.'

His voice rasped, raw and unfamiliar.

'Why? Because you protected me from the kind of gutter photographers who, unlike their welcome, wanted, respectful, carefully selected press colleagues, had never been invited in the first instance? Who had snuck in for the very purpose of causing trouble; pushing me and shoving their cameras into my face and against my stomach? They acted like animals.'

'Exactly like I acted.'

'Nothing like you acted,' she exploded. 'You

were defending me. Anyone could see that. I was scared and you saved me. Besides, it was nothing compared to the way the security guards rough-housed them out of there, or didn't you see that?'

'I know what happened,' he lied. All he could recall was Archie's pinched expression, the fear in her eyes. 'I smashed that guy's camera. I lost control. Just like I lost control in the alley with that kid that night.'

She looked at him like he was crazy. It almost made him want to laugh. Almost.

'Firstly, that *man* in the alley was eight years older than you and looking for trouble. Secondly, you did not break any camera.'

'I grabbed it, it smashed.'

'You took it out of my face. That's all. The photographer tried to snatch it back and some security guy punched it out of his hands and into the post behind him. So forget that one, tainted moment, and remember the rest of the evening,' she whispered. 'Remember how good it was. And don't pull away from me now.'

He wanted so much to believe her. To take what she was offering him. But he couldn't.

If he stood here, enduring the icy waterfall still on his body, then maybe he could withstand the unfamiliar sensations that zipped around his chest. Which made him…feel. And wonder. And yearn.

'I have to. Because if I don't, if we start things, I don't know if I can stop myself around you. And we have to think of the baby.'

'That's an excuse. It might be a factor, even though I've told you I feel ready, and even though you've heard what the doctor has said in every check-up I've had, but it isn't the real reason you push me away.'

'Then what is?'

'That's the part I don't know.' She bit her lip. 'I don't think even you know for sure.'

He just about managed not to flinch. Her words cut closer to the bone than he ever could have imagined. She knew him so well. Maybe too well.

'So,' he bit out, his tongue feeling too big for his mouth, 'if we're done here, perhaps you'd care to leave me to have the rest of my shower in peace?'

The pause stretched out between them.

'Not a chance,' she eventually muttered thickly.

Before he could move, Archie had untied the satin belt and let the dressing gown slide off her shoulders and down over her bump in one easy movement. Far from detracting from the moment, the fact that she was swollen with their baby—with *his* baby—only made her all the sexier.

Still, he should stop this, stop *her*, but she was walking into the shower enclosure with the air of a woman who knew exactly what she was doing and he found it utterly mesmerising.

Worse, though, was that gleam in her eyes. As though she saw a man the rest of the world had missed. As though she saw him the way no one else ever had—a better man. And when she looked at him that way, he so desperately wanted to *be* that man.

Suddenly, she was there, and Kaspar barely had time to turn the temperature up as she closed the last bit of distance separating them. The tips of her fingers grazed over his torso so feather-light he couldn't be sure it she'd actually touched him or if it was just the movement of air, and the wickedest of smiles toyed at the corners of her ridiculously carnal mouth.

What the hell was he meant to do with this woman?

And then her lustrous eyes not leaving his for even a second, Archie dropped to her knees, curled her fingers around his sex, and licked the droplet on the tip, which had nothing to do with the water cascading over him.

He was so nearly lost it took him a moment to move. He tried to step backwards but she was still holding onto him and, honestly, he didn't try very hard.

'Let go, Kaspar,' she murmured. 'Stop trying to control everything and let me take the reins. Just for once.'

And then she took him into her mouth, hot and libidinous. So good it might well have also been immoral. He'd had this done to him before. Many times. A perfect sexual release.

But it had never, ever felt like this. Watching Archie move over him, feeling her hands, her tongue, even the graze of her teeth on him, and also experiencing these complicated emotions swirling around his chest.

Nothing had ever felt so like...*this*.

He gave up trying to think and finally tried to do what she'd instructed. Leaning back on the tiles, because his legs suddenly felt absurdly weak, he buried his hands into her hair and allowed her to take charge.

He wanted her. *Needed* her, even. And whatever he tried to tell himself, he knew it wasn't just the sex. It wasn't just the way she sucked on his head and then slowly drew his thick, solid length deep into her mouth.

It was *her.*

He wanted everything with her. No one else could ever possibly have convinced him to give up the reins like Archie had. And yet here he was, completely at her command. And a part of him thrilled in it.

She started slowly. Deliberately. Setting an unhurried pace as though she was intent on savouring every last moment. She licked him, and sucked him, swirling her tongue over him and using her fingers to apply just the right amount of pressure exactly where he needed it.

He heard himself groan, but he was no more in command of his voice than he was of his body. Instead he was completely and utterly at Archie's mercy and, as though she understood just how much she held the power at this second, she teased him until he thought he was going to die.

And then, suddenly, he was all too shamefully close. As though he was the kind of over-excited adolescent he'd never actually been.

Wrenching himself from her touch, Kaspar ignored her cry of protestation and scooped her up into his arms even as he shut the water off with a flick of his wrist.

'I wasn't finished.'

'I nearly was,' he growled, which only seemed to elicit an exceptionally cheeky grin from Archie.

'That's why I wasn't done. So where are we going instead?'

'Where do you think?' Kaspar demanded, carrying her through to his bedroom and depositing her carefully on the enormous bed.

He'd never wanted anyone the way he wanted Archie. In some dark recess, a voice asked whether he thought he'd ever get enough of her, and alarm bells jangled so loudly there might as well have been a belfry in there.

But he refused to heed them. Instead he muffled the sound.

Still, even as he moved over the bed next to Archie, his hands cradling the beautiful swell to her body, he couldn't help checking.

'Are you sure about this?'

'I've been ready for months,' she groaned, but it was softened with a smile.

The tremble of her body almost sent him over the edge again.

Dropping his head, his lips sought hers, demanding, claiming her as if her mouth was his to take, tilting his head until the fit was perfection itself. As though he could kiss her for ever and never tire of it. Archie looped her arms around his neck, pressing her body, her bump, against him. Not too tight, just enough, as his hands caressed her belly. The fire between them was hotter than ever, threatening to burn out of control at any moment.

Ignoring the deep, heavy throb still clutching at his sex, Kaspar lavished attention on her. When he'd finished kissing her mouth, he moved to her jaw, her ear, her neck, inching his way down her body until she was arching into him and wordlessly begging him for more. When his lips finally alighted on her breast, pulling one exquisite nipple into his mouth as she gasped in pleasure, he at last allowed his hand to wander lower.

She groaned again, her voice an insubstantial whisper.

'Kaspar, I need you to...'

'To what?' he demanded mercilessly, his mouth still full of her soft flesh, his fingers tracing an intricate pattern over her hips.

'To...touch me.'

'I am touching you.' He switched his attentions to her other breast, half enjoying himself, half fighting the urge to pull her on top of him and slide inside her. Finally branding her as his.

Just like he had that first night.

'Not there,' she managed hoarsely.

'Ah.' He allowed his fingers to wander to the top of her thigh, repeating the pattern on the outer side. 'Here?'

'Kaspar,' she moaned, shifting on the bed, subconsciously parting her legs for him, drawing him in.

'Here?' he teased, moving his hand back up until it was stroking her abdomen again.

He lifted his head and she caught his gaze. But this time, instead of the needy sound that threatened to undo him, she pursed her lips into a sinful grin, her hooded eyes were loaded with wanton need.

'Perhaps *you* need a little reminder,' she murmured, moving her own hand down to flutter over him, his body reacting instantly.

He heard the guttural sound, but it took a moment to realise it was him. Her touch was like some exquisite torture. He'd never known it was possible to ache quite like this. Too incredible to be bad yet too painful to be good.

He sought out her core. So slick, and hot,

and ready. His fingers played with her, moving over her at a pace that was faster than he would have liked but he couldn't seem to stop himself, especially at Archie's soft, urgent moans. And then he didn't know who moved first, him or her, but Archie was astride him, one of his hands on her belly and one cupping a heavy, perfect breast.

'Condoms?' she muttered.

'Top drawer.' He jerked his head towards the nightstand, before adding unnecessarily, 'The pack Catherine gave you.'

As though he needed her to know he hadn't bought them for anyone else. In actual fact, he had never brought anyone else into this space.

He watched her open the foil packet, fumbling slightly with her shaking fingers, rolling it down his length with excruciating care. And then Archie was moving over him, guiding him inside as he watched her face for any sign of discomfort. When he finally, *finally* slid inside her wet heat, felt her stretching around him, gripping him tightly despite the slightly shallower depth, he wasn't sure he would last at all. Experimentally, she began to move.

'Okay?' he checked.

She nodded, tentatively increasing the pace,

and it was all Kaspar could do not to move inside her the way his body longed to do. He wanted to move faster, thrust into her deeper and harder until she shattered around him. But he couldn't. Not yet. He tensed with the effort, only realising it when she stroked his jawline, a soft laugh escaping her lips.

'Relax, I'm fine.'

'Sure?'

She nodded again and Kaspar let his hands trail over her body until his thumbs were circling in the soft hair between her legs, her head slumping slightly forward, her breath coming shallow and quick. He dipped lower, playing with her even as he moved inside her, her body thrilling to his touch, tightening around him, moving faster on top of him.

He was so close. So incredibly close. Everything about Archie turned him on in a way he hadn't previously known was possible. And as they moved together in flawless harmony, the initial soft shudders of her body giving way to something far more urgent, and unrelenting, he imagined that this, here now, her, would be all he would ever need.

It was the last thought he had as she finally came apart around him. Her body arched as she surrendered to him, crying out, rocking over him and against his fingers and her hands braced against his chest as though she thought she might otherwise collapse. And just as Archie seemed to start coming down, he changed his rhythm and hurled her over the edge all over again.

This time, when she cried his name, Kaspar couldn't contain himself any longer. He tumbled off the cliff edge with her, better than leaping out of any plane. He released himself into her, and the flames roared and surged through him and he feared they could never be quenched.

Dangerous, even lethal. Yet blissful perfection.

He might have known it could never last.

CHAPTER TWELVE

ARCHIE AWOKE THE next morning to the sun streaming through the curtains, the call of early morning seabirds. And the fact that she was alone. Again.

But this time she didn't worry. Instead she stretched languorously as rarely used muscles lazily grunted their objections, and recalled an hour earlier when she'd awoken to the feel of a warm, solid body behind her.

Kaspar, pressed to her back and his hand cradling her bump. She'd snuggled back, his reaction even in sleep unmistakeable, and tried to drift back off into slumber. As much as they might want to make love again and again, they couldn't. Light and infrequent, that was what Catherine had advised.

At some point, she could just about remember him mentioning going for a run. His attempt to distract his urgent body. And now here she was finally awake, what had to be several hours later. Her ears strained for the sound of the shower or for him in the kitchen, but she heard nothing.

Then again, marathons weren't unusual for Kaspar.

Abruptly she realised what had woken her.

The low, insistent humming of her phone tumbled through the room and though there was no reason at all for the sense of foreboding that flooded through her, she nevertheless shivered under the sheets, despite the warmth of the sunlit room. At this hour, what were the chances it would be the press? Especially after last night's little scene? Kaspar had wordlessly unplugged the phone last night and turned his own cell off, but it wouldn't have taken them much to get her number. She knew what they were like.

So Archie sat, her knees hugged tightly under her chest, waiting. Only breathing again once the drumming finally fell silent.

In.

Out.

In.

Out.

Throwing off the sheets, she crossed the room to look out of the window, seeing the golden beach spread out below her like the most luxurious picnic mat in the world. The sight of Kaspar racing powerfully along the sand, the only figure on the private beach, an unexpected but welcome sight.

Her fingers pressed against the glass as her eyes drank him in, from his muscled thighs to the wide, bare, olive chest that glistened from the exertion, all sending images of last night hurtling around her feverish mind.

But then she caught sight of the expression on his face. Dark, brooding, even angry. And her stomach flip-flopped.

Slowly she backed up, across the room, so that by the time he had powered up the hillside to vault over the small balcony and to the picture-height glass doors, she was already edging to the door. As though, somehow, the distance could silence whatever words he was about to utter. Words, she already knew, she didn't want to hear.

And then he was in the room, stopping dead as he saw her. For one moment she thought she could read frustration, regret in those chocolate depths. And then they were cold, and dark, and forbidding, shutting her out as effectively as anything he could say.

'Kaspar...'

'Have you seen the papers?'

He cut across her and it was almost too much to bear, the way his tone devastated her so easily. So completely.

'How could I have?' She swallowed hard, as if it could buy her more time. 'I've only just woken up.'

'Then allow me to show you.'

His harsh voice sliced her like a hundred scalpel blades, the barely contained fury in no doubt as he stalked past her, flinging the door open and striding down the hallway with all the ire that could have parted the ocean behind them had he changed direction.

It was all Archie could do to scurry behind him, her mind racing too fast for the rest of her thoughts to catch up. Later, she would wonder how she'd had the presence of mind to grab a dressing gown as she left. Short and flimsy as it was, she had no idea at that point how grateful she would be to pull it around her near-naked form in some semblance of self-pride.

'They're emblazoned with ugly photos of the scene from last night,' he continued bitingly, as he entered the study and powered up the laptop, which still sat quietly on the side from his latest round of research. 'Headlines detailing exactly what kind of a volatile, out-of-control man I am. Screaming it for the world to know.'

'They don't know you.' Her breath came out in a whoosh as she moved, actually took a step towards him. 'I do.'

She didn't realise how foolish it was until he snatched his arm away from her outstretched fingers, his eyes darkening with a dangerous glint, the spat-out word a Persian curse that she only now recalled from her youth.

'I do not want your sympathy, Archana.'

She flinched but he barely seemed to notice.

Or perhaps he was deliberately trying to hurt her. To push her away.

'This is exactly who I told you I was; who I told you I wanted to spare our baby from seeing. But you wouldn't listen. You, in your arrogance, thought you could change me.'

'This isn't who you are,' she faltered, but he shot her down.

'This is exactly who I am. I knew it before. It was only my own ego that let me believe your naïve, rose-tinted view of me. You insisted on making us a spectacle, but I was the one who should have known better. Now they have uncovered the story from my past. And so we must both pay the penalty.'

Archie opened her mouth to speak, but then she caught sight of some of the photos he'd been talking about and her lips became too dry, her throat too cracked to form any kind of coherent words. Even if she could have, her heart was clattering in her chest so wildly that she couldn't hope to think straight, couldn't organise the words that jumbled in her head.

One thing leaped out of her more than anything else. One sad, shameful, truth. The expression in her eyes as she stared at Kaspar. The pathetic, unadulterated adoration in her expression.

He was right. She was naïve, and a fool. Nothing more than the silly little girl she'd always been. She'd fallen in love with him. It was there on her face, mocking her, just as Kaspar was mocking her. Once again, she'd fooled herself into believing he'd let her in and here he was reminding her that he never truly would. Perhaps he simply wasn't capable of it.

Kaspar could never be hers. He could never be anyone's. She was a fool for even considering for a moment that he could be.

I deserve better, she chanted desperately, as if

repeating it wildly in her head would be enough to convince her. *I deserve someone who truly loves me*.

And one day, maybe, she might believe that.

So much for the bold, sophisticated Archie she'd tried to kid herself that she was. It was time to grow up and take responsibility. And that meant putting Kaspar Athari into her past once and for all. Or at least the idea of any relationship with him. The truth was that he was her baby's father, she could never truly escape him for the rest of her life.

It was embarrassing how much that thought gave as much comfort as it did torment.

But she didn't have to show it. Lifting her head, Archie forced herself to look him directly in the eyes, her voice conveying a breeziness she hadn't known she possessed.

'You're right.' *Where did that hint of a tight, cold smile come from?* 'I see that now. This marriage was a foolish idea and I apologise for anything I did to make you feel you had little choice but to suggest it.'

Her entire chest wrenched at the words, splitting her apart from her insides out with such force that she had no idea how she managed to stay standing, let alone talking. It was torture not to be able to read a single expression on his face, not that any expression even flickered over Kaspar's unrelenting features. The only reaction at all was the clenched jaw and steady, clear pulse. But even that told her nothing of what was running through his head.

How had she failed to realise before how little she knew him?

'It's the most logical solution.' He offered a curt nod. 'Once the baby is born, we'll get divorced. Blame it on my playboy reputation. The press will be expecting that anyway. You can return to the UK. I'll make the financial arrangements to provide for my child. Once all the furore has died down, which I'm sure won't take too long, we'll decide how I can have contact without turning your life, or our baby's, into a circus.'

She wanted to answer him but she couldn't speak. Her tongue, like her body, was going numb. She could feel herself shutting down.

'I'm going for a run,' he bit out, as if her silence was answer enough. Neither of them mentioned the fact that he'd only just returned from his last one. 'You should pack. I'll let my driver know to pick you up and take you to a hotel near the hospital. It's five-star, and you'll have my suite.'

'No…' she blurted out, but he silenced her with a brief wave of his arm.

'I'll cover the costs.'

As if that was her only objection. Still, it was enough to silence her. Clearly he thought so little of her, what was the point in trying to defend herself?

'Understood.' Her tone sounded nothing like herself.

For a start it didn't betray any of the howling pain that raged inside her.

But then she clutched the flimsy dressing gown around her and was grateful she didn't have nakedness to add to her tearing sense of vulnerability right now.

Too late, Archie realised her mistake. Her action pulled Kaspar up sharply and he raked his hand uncomfortably through his hair.

'Archie…' His voice faltered, something so unfamiliar that for a moment she didn't recognise it for what it was.

And then suddenly she did.

It was *pity*.

Pride slammed into her. He could reject her,

and distance himself, that was his right and there was nothing she could do about it.

But she *could* make damned sure that, on top of everything else, he didn't pity her for her pain.

'What about the press?' she asked.

'What? Does it matter?' He blew out a deep breath. 'Fine, we'll tell them it was the safest option. Closer to hospital, and people would always be around if anything…happened while I was away at work.'

So that was it, she realised as her heart actually seemed to slump inside her drooping ribcage. He had an answer for everything, and she had no more excuses.

She had to be strong. She had a baby to consider now. A future in which someone else was counting on her to make the responsible decisions, and she couldn't ignore that fact. Especially with the way the atmosphere had changed within the room. Heavy. Strained. Foreboding. Even the sunlight getting in on the act since it didn't quite reach this part of the house, and so the shadow left her standing, quite literally, in the cold.

It took more than she could have imagined to shake off the ridiculous notion.

'You're right.' The words sounded thick, heavy, gungy. She forced herself to say them anyway. 'It's best if you go.'

'Then you agree?' he bit out, his gaze boring into her until every fibre of her being trembled under its onslaught.

No, I don't agree, a part of her wanted to scream. But what was the use in arguing?

None of this was enough for her any more. Kaspar was right. Their marriage was a pointless sham. She'd almost convinced herself that if she'd married Joe for practical reasons, then she could certainly stay married to Kaspar. For the sake of their baby. Yet deep down she'd always known it was an entirely different scenario. She'd never *craved* Joe the way she craved Kaspar. Why spend her life watching him, yearning for more, aching for something that could never be?

'I agree.' She thought the words might choke her.

She didn't know whether it was a relief or a disappointment that they didn't. Then, with an offhand dip of his head, Kaspar dismissed her. And she let him. She backed out of the door and walked down the hallway on legs that had no business holding her upright.

Just like that, she'd walked out of another marriage. Or Kaspar had pushed her out. Either way, there was no doubt in her mind that *this* time there would be no getting over it.

He was doing the right thing.

Pounding down the beach, his legs burning from their fight against the soft sand, Kaspar wondered if any amount of beating his body could ever assuage this agony that ripped through his chest.

The sense of failure. Of treachery. Of absolute loss. And it was all his own doing.

The moment he'd seen that photo, the murderous look in his eyes as he'd slammed away that photographer's camera, he'd realised that as much as he might pretend to be a different man—one worthy of someone as innocent and delicate as Archie, one who deserved the way she looked at him, as though he was something special, someone good—he wasn't.

He wasn't special and he wasn't good. He wasn't at all the man she seemed to have convinced herself that he was. He was still the arrogant, out-of-control, emotionally bankrupt teenager he'd been who'd destroyed a man's life all those years ago. All for the sake of a row over an upturned bar stool.

He should have known better that night, just as he should have known better with the photographer at the ball. The press were animals. They'd had no right to jostle Archie as they had, especially not when she was so clearly pregnant. But that didn't mean he could be equally savage and uncontrolled.

And Archie had agreed.

The whole thing only proved that he was as toxic and dangerous as his father had been.

And, for that matter, as manipulative as his mother. Hadn't he pretty much blackmailed Archie into marrying him in the first instance? What kind of a man did that? What sort of an example could that ever set for their child?

Letting her walk away from their marriage was the only honourable thing he could do right now. Set her free. It was shameful that he was having to will himself so hard to keep running. Not turn around and race back up that beach, back to the house, and tell her that she couldn't leave after all.

All the while, a voice inside him grew. A whisper at first. Kaspar could barely hear it even as he pretended not to know what it was saying. It grew in volume, more insistent, more triumphant. He thundered along the beach as though he could outrun it, but the faster he moved the louder it grew. Until, at last, it was a bellow. A roar. It stopped him in his tracks, and it made him swing back round until the only thing he could see—the only thing his eyes would look at—was his beach house, in the distance.

Or, more accurately, the house that had become a *home* ever since Archie had set foot inside. He planted his feet firmly, as though willing himself to ground himself into the sand the way a tree bedded itself into soil. Anything to stop him racing back there and charging in. Telling Archie she couldn't leave. She could never leave. And not just because she was carrying his child. For a long, self-indulgent moment he allowed himself to imagine what she might say. What she might do.

And then he wasn't indulging himself any more because he knew exactly what she would say. She would ask if he loved her. The way she'd wanted to do so many times before, whether she realised it or not. He'd seen it for the first time one morning a few weeks ago. She'd been hovering by the pool, waiting for something, although he suspected she hadn't even realised it herself. It had taken him days to figure out she'd been waiting for him to tell her that he loved her.

And he did.

Unconditionally. Irrevocably.

It was the reason he needed her to leave now. From the instant he'd discovered she was pregnant he'd known he would be there for his child the way his parents had never been there for him. He wanted to give his baby the childhood the Coates family had given to him.

But there had always been something more to it than that. There'd had to be. He would never have proposed such a marriage to any other woman. Only Archie.

Because he wanted her. He wanted *to be with* her.

And if it hadn't been for his ruinous behaviour last night, he might have told her so. Now he knew he owed it to her to let her go. Before the press tainted her with the same poisonous brush with which they were so clearly intending to paint him.

It was only what he deserved.

Just as Archie deserved better. If he really loved her, as he claimed to, then he would let her go, no matter how painful it was to him. Wasn't that what love was supposed to be about? Selfless acts for another person?

All of which ensured that him returning to the house to declare his love for her was the one thing he absolutely *couldn't* do. Kaspar snarled, but only the crashing sea and the squawking gulls bore the brunt of his frustration. And then, with what felt like a superhuman effort, he whirled around and ran, sinking furiously into the sand as though he might leave his footprints there for ever.

He had no idea how long he kept running, or how far he went. But when he finally lifted his head he was no longer on the beach, he wasn't even anywhere near the ocean, and the morning sun was on the other side of the sky as people began to emerge for their early evening revelries.

He'd been running all day. Around in circles. Just as his head was doing.

Only then did Kaspar finally turn back and head for the house which would no longer ever be a home to him.

CHAPTER THIRTEEN

FOR THREE DAYS she had stayed cooped up in the hotel room, wallowing in her misery, which wasn't easy as she wasn't a person generally accustomed to self-pity. She hadn't wallowed when her marriage to Joe had ended, or when she'd lost the baby, or even when her father had died. She'd tried to be strong, and stoic, and soldier on.

And look where that had got her.

She hadn't actually pushed through all the grief and the heartache, at all. She'd simply been sucked even deeper down into it. The more she'd struggled to pretend she was fine, the faster she'd sunk, a little like trying to fight when the quicksand already had an unbreakable hold.

So Archie had decided that maybe if she wallowed this time, gave in to the wealth of misery that swirled around her, she could exhaust all her sorrow and make it out the other side.

It wasn't working. Because the more she indulged her sadness, the more her brain started whirring again, wondering if she wasn't perhaps missing something. Second-guessing herself.

Her mobile phone rang for the umpteenth time. An unknown number every time. She'd learned not to answer it after the first few times, when the media's questions had been fired at her before she'd even finished saying hello. But this number had a Swiss code in front of it.

'Archana?'

Archie stopped, any response lodged in her throat.

'It's me,' he faltered uncertainly. 'Joe?'

'Yes.' She bit back the additional, *I know who you are.*

'I just thought I should...' He cleared his throat and she could imagine him, rigid and upright.

A neat shirt and tie under a round-necked wool jumper. She couldn't imagine why he was calling. She couldn't imagine it was to revel in her public humiliation. Of all her ex-husband's flaws, taking delight in someone else's misfortune had never been one of them.

Archie sucked in a breath, waiting for him to continue. Not wanting to reveal her confusion.

'I saw your photo in the paper. I...wanted to call and congratulate you.'

'Sorry?' The word escaped before she could stop it. A squeak of shock.

'The baby. And that you look...happy,' he continued awkwardly, clearly mistaking her response. 'In love.'

The words didn't come easily to him. They never had. But she knew him well enough to know the sentiment was genuine.

'No...' she managed, her tongue struggling to wrap itself around any form of coherent response. 'You've got it wrong.'

'Archana.' He silenced her quickly, and she could hear the rueful smile in his voice. 'Please don't do me the disservice of trying to spare my feelings, however well intentioned.'

'I—'

'You love him. That's plain to see from the photos. Had you once, ever, looked at me in that way...' He tailed off, clearing his throat again. 'Well, perhaps if I had treated you to the same...passion as Kaspar Athari does, maybe you *would* have looked at me in that way. It's clear that he loves you in a way that I never did. Or could. The way you deserve to be loved.'

Archie wasn't sure what he said after that. She heard him speaking, as far from his usual reserved manner as she thought she'd probably ever heard him, but she was too busy hurrying across the suite to retrieve her laptop, to fire it up and find those images she'd refused to look at since that morning in Kaspar's study.

By the time Joe ended the short conversation, she was sinking down on the dining chair, staring at the truth, which had been there all along—only she'd been too caught up in the puppy-dog expression on her own face to see it.

Only this time that wasn't what she saw. It was as though all the scales had dropped from her eyes, taking with them all the preconceived notions she'd been carrying around. Suddenly, she could see what Joe could see. What he'd been trying, in his typically restrained way, to say. What the rest of the world could see.

A couple so patently in love with each other that it shone out from the page.

She didn't look like a pathetic, lost puppy. She looked like a woman—an expectant mother—very much in control of her feelings. And it showed a man who, even as he dealt efficiently and necessarily with the unmistakeable threat to her well-being, never once let his hot, possessive gaze leave her. As though she was the only important thing in the room. In the entire world.

How had she failed to see it before?

It was time to go and claim her husband. The father of her unborn baby. She wanted a life with him, as a proper family. It was the reason why she'd jumped on that plane to the States those brief few months before, whether she'd realised it or not.

Archie stood with more purpose than she'd felt in a long time, striding across the expansive space to snatch up the phone and call Reception.

'It's Archana Athari, from the Princess Suite,' she began unnecessarily. 'I would like a taxi, please. To take me to me…home.'

It was done. In that instant she felt lighter, and more optimistic.

She could call Kaspar's driver, of course, but he might call Kaspar, and she didn't want to alert her husband to her change of plans.

He loved her. She knew that with a bone-deep certainty that she'd never realised existed in her before now. But she also knew that Kaspar was proud, and stubborn. He had pushed her away because he truly, incredibly, believed that her life was better without him in it. He couldn't be more wrong, which was exactly what she intended to tell him. He wouldn't want to hear it at first, but she didn't care. She could convince him, however long it took. Still, it wouldn't hurt to stack the deck in her favour as much as possible, and that included giving herself the element of surprise. If he knew she was at his house, he might suddenly decide he had more pressing matters and stay at the hospital, but if he got home to find her already there, he could hardly just walk out.

She threw everything into her suitcases with lightning speed. It wasn't really difficult since she hadn't unpacked the bags Kaspar had sent over that first day. Possibly that should tell her everything she needed to know. And then she opened the door to the hallway ready for the bellhop.

As Archie checked the room over for anything she might have forgotten, she wasn't prepared for the first contraction that gripped her with almost no warning. Neither was she prepared for her husband to walk through the door as though she'd summoned him by her very thoughts.

'Kaspar…?' She gaped, her mind struggling to work.

Thirty-five weeks? She still had a month to go. They had to be Braxton-Hicks, right?

'There are probably a million ways I could do this that would make the moment romantic, and meaningful, and everything you could want,' Kaspar plunged on, oblivious. 'But right now I can't think of a single one of them. So I'll just say it as simply and as clearly as I can. I love you, Archie. Not as the mother of my child, but for *you*. I love, and I'm in love with, you.

'I thought I was broken, and beyond repair, but you found a way to put me back together, and although I may not always show it in the right way, I promise you that I'm learning and if you give me another chance I'll ensure you never regret it. Not for the rest of time.'

The pain was spreading through her abdomen even as her heart felt as though it was sprouting wings ready to take flight. Whoever knew it was possible to feel so frightened and yet so elated all in the same moment?

'Archie…'

'I love you too, you idiot,' she managed. A

combination of clenched teeth and a joyful sob. 'But do you...do you think we could do this later? Only... I think the baby is on his way.'

One day, she knew, she would remember the look of marvel on his face. She would remember this feeling that she was ready for anything, and she would remember this moment as the perfect start to the new chapter of her life.

'Of course our baby is on its way.' The smile was wide, his eyes gleaming, and a look of almost triumph was in his gaze, making her feel very powerful. 'She clearly approves of the moment and can't wait another few weeks to join us in our new future.'

EPILOGUE

SHUFFLING FORWARD ON her bottom, Archana Athari took the hook from the front of her harness and fitted her static line through the eye on the floor of the tiny light aircraft, pulling hard to ensure it was locked securely in place before Kaspar double-checked the line for her.

'Are you ready?' Kaspar called over the roar of the engines and the wind. 'Remember, aside from our one tandem jump together four years ago, you haven't jumped in a decade. And a three-year-old and a one-year-old make the most critical audiences ever.'

'I know.' She grinned at the thought of her son and daughter down on the ground, waiting for them both. 'According to your eldest, those go-carts you made them last week are ruined because you put pictures of the wrong animated films on the side.'

She had no idea whether Kasper heard her or not but it didn't matter. He understood anyway, and his lazy, sexy grin of response sent a wave of adrenalin coursing through her, just like it always did.

Sliding forward, still on her bottom, to the door of the plane, Archie stuck her feet out and leaned forward. The blur of the ground rushing by a few thousand feet below snatched her breath away. For a moment she froze.

'Go!' he bellowed.

And then she offered Kaspar a cheeky wink, yelling against the rushing wind, 'Race you to the bottom!'

Grasping the doorframe with one hand and the metal spar with the other, Archie pulled herself out of the aircraft, twisted and let go. Gravity took over.

Every single thought went from her head.

Spread-eagled in the air, her back arched as she fought for stability, the plane seemed to disappear in seconds, its increasing height above her the only indication that she was falling. And then the jolt of the ripcord opened her chute and reminded her of where she was and what she was supposed to be doing.

One-one-thousand.

Two-one-thousand.

Three-one-thousand.

Archie looked up and her heart slammed into her chest. The canopy hadn't fully deployed.

I probably counted too quickly. I hope I counted too quickly. What did they say about cutting away? I don't want to have to do that. I'll count again and then I'll act.

Her mouth parched and her chest hammering, Archie reached up for the guides that would help her steer for landing. And when she looked again, even before she had chance to count a second time, the parachute opened fully with an ear-splitting *crack!*

And then the complete, utter silence.

She felt weightless. Perhaps not *being in space* weightlessness, but certainly as though she was just floating down, the sky going on for ever around her.

She'd finally done it. Not just for her young son, and younger daughter—who were waiting down on the ground with a very pregnant Katie, and who had been going on about wanting to see her skydive ever since they'd seen the photo of that first tandem jump of their mummy and daddy—but also for herself and for her father.

'Here's to you, Dad,' she whispered. 'I finally got everything I ever dreamed of.'

Peace flowed through her. Her life was so very different from the last time she'd tried this and it was all thanks to Kaspar, and Darius and baby Yasmin. She felt more complete than she had ever imagined possible.

For what felt like an eternity she simply drank it in.

Without warning, a figure dropped in front of her, arms and legs outstretched to slow their fall but, without an open chute, they were still dropping considerably faster than her. He might be too far away to impede her jump but she didn't need to see his face to know who it was.

Kaspar.

And, by his thumbs-up gestures, he was clearly taking her challenge seriously. Her stomach knotted with a kind of anticipation, a thrill, then he was gone, his legs straightening back and his arms pinned to his sides as he tipped his body to dive lower.

But he knew what he was doing and Archie knew he would be safe. The adrenalin junkie at his extreme was long gone. Replaced instead by a fun-loving, proud husband and father, although still—always—her Surgeon Prince of Persia.

Archie laughed into the silence. A rich, happy

sound. Then she let the wind carry her gently down to earth.

She should have known that Kaspar would beat her. By the time she'd gathered up her parachute and made her way across the field, he was already heading back with a feverishly clapping three-year-old on his shoulders and a one-year-old glued to his chest.

'Wow, Mummy.' The awestruck voice carried easily with its childish lilt. 'It was good? Yes or no?'

'Yes, baby. It was very good. But being back here with you is even better.'

And it was true. Her little family was perfect. Everything she could have ever dreamed of having.

Her past, her present and her future, all rolled into one.

* * * * *

LET'S TALK

Romance

For exclusive extracts, competitions
and special offers, find us online:

- f facebook.com/millsandboon
- ⊙ @millsandboonuk
- 🐦 @millsandboon

Or get in touch on 0844 844 1351*

For all the latest titles coming soon,
visit millsandboon.co.uk/nextmonth